A Big Break

"You're going to be *Lacey*?" Charles asked, hands on each side of his face.

Reese tried to be calm. She nodded. "The character is Teresita. She sings solos in 'America' *and* 'I Feel Pretty'— and she has lines—*and* a featured dance bit!"

Charles looked at her. She looked at him.

"AGGHHHHH!"

She couldn't see. She couldn't feel her feet touching the ground. This was *IT*—she had made it. Okay, it was only for rehearsals, but it was a role, a real role, *in a professional theater*!

"AGGHHHHH!"

Charles was screaming, too, almost as loud as Reese. His face was red. They were jumping together, his arms around her, right in front of the theater exit. Who cared if people saw them?

Drama Club Book 4:

Summer Stars

Peter Lerangis

speak
An Imprint of Penguin Group (USA) Inc.

SPEAK

Published by the Penguin Group

Penguin Group (USA) Inc., 345 Hudson Street, New York, New York 10014, U.S.A.
Penguin Group (Canada), 90 Eglinton Avenue East, Suite 700,
Toronto, Ontario, Canada M4P 2Y3 (a division of Pearson Penguin Canada Inc.)
Penguin Books Ltd, 80 Strand, London WC2R 0RL, England
Penguin Ireland, 25 St Stephen's Green, Dublin 2, Ireland
(a division of Penguin Books Ltd)
Penguin Group (Australia), 250 Camberwell Road, Camberwell, Victoria 3124, Australia
(a division of Pearson Australia Group Pty Ltd)
Penguin Books India Pvt Ltd, 11 Community Centre,
Panchsheel Park, New Delhi - 110 017, India
Penguin Group (NZ), 67 Apollo Drive, Rosedale, North Shore 0632, New Zealand
(a division of Pearson New Zealand Ltd.)
Penguin Books (South Africa) (Pty) Ltd, 24 Sturdee Avenue,
Rosebank, Johannesburg 2196, South Africa

Registered Offices: Penguin Books Ltd, 80 Strand, London WC2R 0RL, England

Published by Speak, an imprint of Penguin Group (USA) Inc., 2008

1 3 5 7 9 10 8 6 4 2

LIBRARY OF CONGRESS CATALOGING-IN-PUBLICATION DATA

Lerangis, Peter.
Summer stars / Peter Lerangis.
p. cm. — (Drama Club ; bk. 4)
Summary: During a summer stock production of "West Side Story,"
starring a popular young television star, tensions mount both on and off
the stage between members of Long Island's Ridgeport High School Drama
Club and a rival group of interns.
ISBN 978-0-14-241116-2 (pbk.)
[1. Theater–Fiction. 2. Long Island (N.Y.) — Fiction.] I. Title.
PZ7.L558Sv 2008   [Fic]–dc22

Speak ISBN 978-0-14-241116-2

Printed in the United States of America

Prologue

CALL ME DANCERSLUT.

Everyone does.

It's my screen name. I picked it way back in middle school, to the dismay of my parents. I didn't really know what I was doing. A few years later I thought of changing it, but by then it was too late. Charles Scopetta likes to say that I "became the name"—but that's Charles. Actually the name became me.

I could have just left it at "Dancer," because, duh, I live and breathe dance—ballet, jazz, tap, hip-hop, modern, studying since the age of three, etc., etc, etc. But "slut" makes the whole thing crunchy. My parents hate it. They say that everyone will "expect a certain something." They don't see the joke. It's about attitude, hello? It's about leaving your audience wanting more. Everyone in school knows this—well, pretty much everyone—and no one takes it seriously. That'll be my epitaph—*Here lies Reese Van Cleve, who no one took seriously.*

I like it that way, a lot. Which makes me a freak, in my circle. Not-being-taken-seriously gets my friend Brianna Glaser totally bent out of shape. Harrison Michaels, too. People expect a lot from them. If Brianna doesn't get into, like, Yale, everyone will shake their heads sadly and she will be devastated. If Harrison doesn't win a Tony Award for Best Actor on Broadway, same thing. But between you and me, they have it all backward. Here's the secret: when no one takes you seriously, no one expects anything. No one bothers to block your path to the top. So when you get there, they haven't even been looking.

And that'll be the last part of my epitaph: . . . *whom no one took seriously, but who got everything she wanted.*

I've known my destiny since sixth grade. May 14, to be exact. The Day I Danced for Max Risdal. I was third girl from the left in the finale of the Roberta P. O'Neill Middle School Talent Show here in Ridgeport, Long Island. It was the twenty-seventh and last item on the program, and by that time the parents and teachers were bored and cranky. We were dancing and lip-synching to a Madonna song—but all I could think about was this: sitting in the front row was my friend Jeannette Risdal's uncle Max, the Broadway casting director! I nearly barfed up my lunch with anxiety. Afterward he came backstage to congratulate us. He was tall and old and skinny, with a gold silk kerchief around his neck and a British accent. Later on I overheard him say to a parent: "There is exahhctly *one child* on that stage who will hahhve a Broadway career. But of courrrse, I cahhhn't say who . . ."

Of courrrrse, I knew who.

Moi!

Already I thought I was pretty special. I could dance *en pointe* and execute a perfect triple time step, woo-hoo! But now Max Risdal had discovered me. I was anointed. Nothing was going to stop me from being a Star.

The gold kerchief should have been a tip-off, but in sixth grade my Cheeseball Alert was not fully developed. The next year, when I finally figured out that Jeannette was lying—that Uncle Max wasn't a casting director but only a doorman at an off-Broadway theater, the guy who guards the stars from tourists—I didn't care. By that time I had my screen name. I had my image and my goal. My fate was sealed.

Now I'm a rising senior at Ridgeport High School, and I choreograph the plays for the Drama Club. You may have seen me in the Arts and Leisure section of the *New York Times* recently, in an article about RHS and our fabulous, mega-budget musicals. In the photo I was center stage with a huge grin, soaring through the air in mid-*jeté*. Charles, our set designer, calls me a spotlight whore—which I suppose is true, but no one gets to be a star by being shy. Especially in our town, where theater is the whole world. Everyone knows someone who knows someone who does something on Broadway. The school lobby is plastered with cast photos dating back a century. We call it the Wall of Fame, and it includes a "shrine" to our graduates who have made it on Broadway. To be a success in theater here, you really have to kick ass.

This year was the DC's best ever. We did three awesome plays—a small musical in the fall, *Godspell*; the Big Spring Musical, *Grease*; and an original nonmusical R-rated play called *Early Action* by our resident student genius, Chip Duggan, which was so hot it nearly got our faculty director, Mr. Levin, fired.

All year long I worked hard on the dances and movement. I helped direct, too, even though I didn't get credit. I played one of the roles in *Godspell*. I made everybody laugh. I loosened up our president, Harrison Michaels, who can be a pain in the butt. I was shot down for the major leads in the last two plays, but I didn't complain. Complaining is useless, when you think about it. It just annoys people. So I just did my job, staged the dances, and kept my eyes open.

I knew my time would come. I could wait.

And plan. And become the best dancer I could possibly be.

This summer, for instance, I was going to study with a new ballet teacher who had been a principal dancer for the Kirov Ballet. My mom was pushing me to get a job, of course—or take a class that would somehow "enhance my competitiveness for colleges." All my friends were doing one or the other—Brianna was going to work at her mom's hedge fund, Harrison in his dad's diner, Casey Chang at the hospital where her mom is a nurse. Dashiell Hawkins, our tech guy, was going to math camp, and Chip Duggan, who is, btw, Casey's boyfriend, was studying something at

Johns Hopkins. Only Charles was vague about his plans, and my big goal for the summer was to convince him to take ballet. He laughed in my face, of course.

Nobody saw what was coming. Especially what was coming for me. That's the way it is when people don't expect much from you.

But that was the summer that Shawn Nolan came to town. And the world as I knew it completely exploded.

Part 1
Something's Coming

June 20

1

"GOD, IS HE HOT," SAID REESE VAN CLEVE, carefully eyeing the wide-shouldered guy with the killer smile and reddish-brown hair who at that moment could have said "Ow" and drawn a stampede of twenty-seven highly concerned females.

Shawn Nolan.

I am looking at THE Shawn Nolan. Just the thought of it made a little pinprick of wow sprout from somewhere near her brain and race down her body. Or maybe it was the effects of a day in the sun. School was out, and priorities being what they were, today had been devoted to the perfect tan.

He looked better in person than he did on *Posse Malibu*, Reese decided. His hair was lighter, his face redder, frecklier, more human. And that smile—how did you describe a smile like that? He had been in town awhile— his little autograph signing at the Ridgeport Harbor Festival in late May was the reason practically no one had attended the first performance of *Early Action*—but this was the first time she had seen him. Surrounded by a tight knot of grinning people in linen suits and summer dresses, he managed to gracefully grab a shrimp hors d'oeuvre from a waitress who was so nervous she nearly dropped her tray.

He was laughing politely at a joke told by Professor Glaser, father of her friend Brianna. The Glasers were the hosts of this party, a fund-raiser for the local summer-stock theater in Sandy Shores, two towns to the east. They had rented a huge, circus-size tent with blue and white stripes (matching the theater decor), a band, a dance floor, a buffet, a bar, and round wooden tables. A group of waiters circulated with hot food. They looked like high school kids, but Reese didn't recognize any of them. Overhead was a massive banner that read The SANDY SHORES PLAYHOUSE—FIFTY YEARS AND COUNTING . . .

Because Professor and Mrs. Glaser were Playhouse board members—and their backyard was the site of the party—Brianna and her best friends were all invited. Which meant all of the Drama Club officers. Plus Kyle Taggart. Brianna always found an excuse to involve Kyle, now only the second hunkiest guy under the big top. Arguably.

"I told you Shawn was hot," Brianna said. She sipped a nonalcoholic mojito, courtesy of the reasonably cute bartender, who *might* have believed Brianna's claim that she was twenty-one if her mom hadn't been paying his salary that night.

"Definitely hot," added Casey Chang in her quiet, appraising way.

"Working on our vocabulary builders today, are we?" said Charles Scopetta as he finished a mushroom-bacon-and-cheese mini-quiche, one of four appetizers crowding a small napkin in his hand. "We've nailed *hot*, I think, so perhaps we can move on to—"

"Pompous," suggested Harrison Michaels. "Diminutive. Bland. Vapid."

"Oh, please," Reese said. Harrison was so easy to read. Of all the DC officers, he was the most like her. Driven, ambitious, calculating, talented. But *much* more intense—which made him so much fun to play with. "How about *jealous*, Greek boy?"

Harrison made a face. "Why would I even feel an ounce of envy for the star of an embarrassing turkey of a TV show?"

"Because he has everything you don't have," Reese said, "except maybe for this nice butt."

He tried to jerk away, but her pinch nabbed a good solid chunk.

"Two points, Reester!" said Kyle, heading toward them with three drinks. Dashiell Hawkins, the DC's tech guru, trailed behind him. Kyle was the Original DC Hottie, a six-three football lug with the voice of an angel and a stage presence that vacuumed eyeballs. "Yo, the girl bartender asked for my autograph. She insisted I was the guy from *Hunk Island*."

"Girl bartender?" Brianna said with a sneer.

"Is that wrong?" Kyle replied. "Bartenderette?"

Brianna gave him a withering, how-can-you-be-so-clueless look. "The point is, you're being sexist. Would you ever use the term *boy bartender*?"

"Not if it's a girl, and you want a drink, and she thinks you're a TV star!" Kyle said with a laugh. "I signed her arm. We're getting together after this fund-raiser."

"Kyle, you are shameless," Charles said.

Kyle nodded enthusiastically. "Totally."

"Unsurprisingly I was not misidentified as Taye Diggs," said Dashiell, taking one of Kyle's drinks. "I hope these are quality Roy Rogerses."

"Um," Casey whispered, gazing furtively into the corner. "He's looking at us—Shawn!"

And so he was. Brianna's mom and dad, flanking the TV star, were nodding toward the DC, pointing them out to Shawn.

Reese instantly shifted to one hip and cocked her head, allowing her eyes to meet his briefly, noncommittally, and then wander away. As if she couldn't have cared less and her heart was not beating at seven thousand thumps per minute.

"*Harrison, do not pick your nose,*" said Charles. "Some of our senses of humor have changed since second grade."

"God, Harrison, don't embarrass us in front of Shawn," Reese said through gritted teeth.

Harrison laughed. "You're on a first-name basis?"

"Shut up," Reese shot back. "I'm just enjoying the visuals."

A tray of sizzling appetizers materialized in front of them, attached to the arm of a waiter with small piercing brown eyes, a sharp nose, a jutting jaw, and luxuriously long blond hair tied back in a ponytail. He was cute in a rough way, maybe sixteen or seventeen.

"Darlings!" Brianna's mom swept toward them, nearly knocking over the waiter's plate. "Oops, so sorry. Brianna, sweetie, please come over and meet Shawn when you have a chance. And Stuart Bishop, the director." She lowered her voice meaningfully. "They want to expand the *West Side Story* cast, you know—beyond the professional actors they've cast out of New York City. Maybe a couple more Jets, a couple of Sharks. It's *très* big-budget now, and *of course* I told him about all the unbelievable *young* acting talent right under this tent!"

"I imagine he's heard of Ridgeport High School," Dashiell said.

Mrs. Glaser smiled. "He has now," she said over her shoulder.

The waiter cocked his head, giving her a curious look.

"What are these?" Dashiell asked, eyeing the hors d'oeuvres.

"Huh?" Ponytail said. "Oh. Nantucket bay scallops. Wrapped in bacon."

Seven hands reached in and quickly emptied the platter.

"You're welcome," he murmured dully before anyone had a chance to thank him, then ducked away.

Charles watched him go. "Charming. Good people skills."

"He must be one of the summer interns from Sandy Shores High School," Brianna said. "Mom insisted the caterers hire them."

"Interns?" Reese said. "The Playhouse lets high school kids act in the shows?"

Brianna shook her head. "No. It's a professional theater, cast out of New York. Once in a while, if they're stuck, they let local amateurs play small roles. The interns work on sets, lighting, costumes—for free. No pay for the whole season, all five shows. Which is why Mom pays them for this event."

"Thoughtful," Casey remarked.

Brianna shrugged. "That's Mom. She grew up near the Playhouse and interned there in high school, so she knows how they feel."

"Your mom grew up in *Sandy Shores*?" Reese said. That was a shock. Maybe it was her wardrobe, the endless haute couture dresses that you never saw twice. Maybe it was the fact that she ran a hedge fund, or that you saw her face nearly every week in the *Wall Street Journal*. Or the string of degrees—B.A., M.A, M.B.A., Ph.D. Whatever, you did not expect the hometown of Evangeline Rogere-Glaser to be a place of tiny houses, strip malls, and bait-and-tackle shops.

"Queen Glaser's story was told in *Forbes* magazine, doll—*helloooo, I'll take some of those!*" Charles said, waving at another intern waiter, a girl with close-cropped black curly hair who was carrying a tray of steaming food. "The title was 'Rags to Riches in Ridgeport.'"

As Charles reached for an hors d'oeuvre, the girl curtsied. With an ironic smile, she chirped, "I'm Callie, your waitress from Rags."

Charles, who had managed to stuff his mouth during the remark, shrugged apologetically.

The Glasers were gesturing with vigor now, signaling Brianna and her friends to come join them. The little crowd around Shawn had grown. The Drama Club's faculty adviser, Mr. Levin, was there, too, standing near a balding potbellied guy with a scraggly reddish-gray beard who was holding a huge, full, salted margarita.

Kyle, Charles, Harrison, Dashiell, and Casey all threaded their way through the crowd as Reese stumbled along after Brianna, who would not let go of her hand.

As they neared the Glasers, Reese tripped over a root, lurching forward and stopping herself only by clomping her foot to the ground.

She jerked upright and came face to face with Shawn Nolan.

"I, uh, do my own stunts," she blurted.

The flawless sculpture that doubled as Shawn's face burst into an openmouthed laugh. "Ha! Jennifer Garner, right?"

"Huh?" Reese said.

He was perfect.

"At the Oscars—or was it the Emmys?" Shawn said. "When she tripped over her gown? Didn't she say that?"

"Oh. Right," Reese said—which was marginally more

intelligent than the second "Huh?" that was at the tip of her tongue.

His eyes were a deep blue, flecked with green. His skin, slightly pinked by the sun, seemed to be made of some smooth sculptural material. And his cheekbones were like suspension bridges, as if lifted by some secret rigging inside his jaw. She remembered arguing about him last year with a friend who said he was too normal-looking—but now she knew. Stars were stars for a reason. They were a different kind of normal.

"Shawn, this is our daughter, Brianna," said Mrs. Glaser, "and her friends from the Ridgeport High Drama Club. Harrison and Brianna are president and vice president—and top-notch actors both! Now, Charles here is the genius behind the sets, Dashiell is the tech person from heaven, and Reese—"

"The choreographer," Shawn said.

"Oh? You know them, then?" Professor Glaser bellowed heartily.

Shawn shrugged, his dark blue eyes pinning Reese. "Just figured she had to be. The most coordinated one is always the one who trips."

It was by far the sweetest thing Reese had heard in days. "Thanks," she said.

"And this is Stuart Bishop," Mr. Levin said, nodding toward the bearded man, who had downed most of his margarita. "He's an old pal from Carnegie-Mellon. He'll be directing Shawn, who will be playing the lead role of Tony in the playhouse's first production of the summer, West Side Story."

"*If* I can hit the high notes," Shawn said, running his fingers through hair thick with gel. "I'm working with a vocal coach in Ridgeport. I used to sing, in my high school. But just in the chorus. I wasn't very good."

That's what it was about the smile. His mouth was a little lopsided, which seemed to steer his face away from perfection. And made him absolutely beautiful.

"I can help you," Harrison spoke up. "I mean, if you need it."

"Harrison has a powerful lyric baritone voice, with great technique for a high school kid," Mr. Levin said.

"Dude," Shawn said, with a wide-open, friendly lopsided smile, "you should try out for the play." He glanced at Mr. Bishop. "I can see him as a Shark, right?"

"He's the right type," Mr. Bishop said diplomatically.

"These Drama Club kids would be great assets to any theater company," Mr. Levin said, "with the training and experience they've had."

As Mr. Bishop took another hearty swig, emptying his margarita, Professor Glaser reached for the glass. "Let me refresh that for you. . . ."

"What do you think, Stuart?" Mrs. Glaser asked, with her most charming cocktail-party smile.

Mr. Bishop cast her a wary glance. "Well, we do want to expend—ex*pand* the cast a bit," he said, his words a little slurry. "I did have older actors in mind, though. I'm sure there are some locals—"

"I always thought actors should be the same age as the characters onstage," Shawn piped up. "It sucks to have, like, a thirty-two-year-old playing a high school kid. I see that a lot onstage."

"Mmm. Well, local auditions are this Monday, June twenty-third," Mr. Bishop said.

"Wait," Brianna said, barely containing the shock in her voice, "are you saying we *can* audition for roles?"

"Unless you're more interested in backstage possibilities—internships," Mr. Bishop said with a vague hopefulness, "in which case speak to our producer, G. Sullivan Little. He's the tall fellow over by the buffet table."

"But . . ." Brianna eyed her mom. "My summer job, at the Krok Fund . . ."

"We could rearrange things, dear," Mrs. Glaser said cheerily. "Stuart, you are *such* a love!"

Mr. Bishop cast a somewhat droopy eye toward Brianna. "You realize, of course, that the audition is just for this one show. Not for the rest of the season. *West Side Story* lasts for two weeks only. Then we have a magic show coming in for two weeks, followed by three shows with smaller casts. I believe we have found enough actors for those shows already."

"Fine," Brianna squeaked.

"Totally!" Reese agreed. She had to control herself before a squeal burst up from her toes and tore through the ridiculous grin on her face. *Auditioning*, for a professional theater production?

Awesome. *Amazing!* She knew it. She *knew* something like this would happen.

"Easy, Lindsay Lohan, you're not cast yet," Harrison murmured.

Reese stepped on his foot. Hard.

"What if we want to be interns, not actors? Can we stay for the whole summer?" Charles asked.

"You'll have to take that up with Mr. Little," Mr. Bishop said, reaching for a jacket pocket and missing the jacket entirely. "Uh, let me write down your names. I'll give the list to our stage manager, Carol Richards. Check with her when you arrive. Ten A.M. sharp. We have very, very tight security . . ."

Mrs. Glaser discreetly handed Mr. Bishop a business card, and as Harrison recited the DC names, Mr. Bishop wrote them on the back.

Harrison grasped Mr. Bishop's free hand and shook it. "Thanks. This is nice of you. You know, I played Bernardo in a summer-camp production up in the Finger Lakes."

"What roles are open?" Brianna asked.

"Is it going to be a singing or a dancing call?" Reese blurted out.

"I wonder if I can cancel math camp," Dashiell murmured. "I would hate to miss this opportunity. Although that's an opportunity also. And I am scheduled to leave tomorrow . . ."

"Math camp?" Charles asked.

"It's in Detroit this year," Dashiell replied.

"And you're going *voluntarily*?" Charles said.

Brianna's dad returned with a fresh margarita, which Mr. Bishop grabbed eagerly. "Don't be concerned with dressing up, acting the right way, et cetera," he said. "I'm sure you kids know this, but do read the show's script. The story's based on *Romeo and Juliet*—"

"Set in the 1950s in the streets of New York City between white and Puerto Rican gang members," Brianna added.

"The Jets and Sharks," Reese said.

"Originally it was entitled *East Side Story*," Dashiell began. "About Jews and Catholics. However, the creative team came to the realization that the show had already been done. Its title was—"

"Uh, thanks, Dashiell," Harrison said, with his best *Not Now* look. "Thanks."

"Er, for the audition bring us your best eight bars," Mr. Bishop said, "standard show tune, and be prepared to dance . . . mamba, sambo . . . I mean, mambo, samba . . ."

As he slipped away, toward the bar, Reese leaped from the ground. She came down into a big Drama Club group hug.

"Today Sandy Shores, tomorrow the Tonys, babe!" Charles shouted.

Shawn Nolan was laughing.

Reese held on to the bar to keep from floating away.

2

"HOW DO I LOOK, *CHICA?*" REESE SAID, FLAVORING
her words with a Puerto Rican accent.

Brianna climbed out of the car, shaking. She had never
been this nervous about an audition. She watched Reese
spin around, her frilly fan skirt flying.

They had all spent the night online with each other,
working out strategies to get out of summer commitments,
detailing the occasional screaming fight with parents, etc.
In the end, most of the moms and dads agreed on a wait-
and-see attitude. (Harrison's Greek dad, who was usually
the least flexible, was "prouded for" his son and agreed to
rework his busboy schedule.) Brianna, Reese, and Harrison
would audition; Casey would ask about interning as an
assistant stage manager; and Charles would volunteer for

props and sets. After much deliberation, Dashiell decided to go ahead with his math camp plans.

"You look just like a gangster girlfriend of a Shark," Brianna told Reese. "Which is what Mr. Bishop said *not* to do. We're not supposed to dress up. And you are, by the way, *not* Puerto Rican."

"*Mi madre*," Reese said, "*esta Milta Rosas Van Cleve.* Born in San Juan."

Harrison, who had driven them all there, was wearing a variation of his Danny Zuko outfit from *Grease*—high-waisted jeans with rolled-up cuffs, white socks, a T-shirt with a pack of fake cigs tucked into the sleeve, black Converse sneakers. Which was also a little over the top— but at least it was neutral. It could go either way, white-boy Jet or Latino Shark. "Reese, you'll be in trouble if they're looking for a Jet girl," he said.

"Don't underestimate the power of suggestion, *hijo*." Reese turned her shoulder to him, flipping her red hair in his direction, and headed across the parking lot toward the theater.

"Personally I think you look amazing, *kiddando*," Charles said, falling into step with her.

"No such word," Reese replied.

"Kiddando is in the script," Charles replied. "I read it, while I was ignoring all your IMs."

"Actually, I was Googling a lot, too," Brianna said. "And I read that the writers were totally embarrassed by stuff like the word *kiddando*—also some of the lyrics to 'I Feel Pretty' and 'America.' It took them a while to realize they were using dumb-white-guy stereotypes."

"A walk with you is a tutorial in drama, La Glaser," Charles said. "Perhaps you can continue Professor Dashiell's lecture on the show's history. I for one would be fascinated."

Brianna shut up. She was talking too much. She always did that when she was petrified. Already at least a dozen cars were parked in the lot, and more were gliding in by the second. Many of the people climbing out were dressed in fifties-style clothing, the girls stunning, the guys angular and tough-looking. Everyone looked at least in their midtwenties. Who *were* they? Who knew there were so many aspiring professional actors in Long Island? Most of them walked like Reese, with their legs turned out (which Brianna hated because it announced *Behold, dancer*).

The more dancers she saw, the more Brianna's calves ached. On Reese's advice, she had taken four dance classes over the weekend—ballet, jazz, and two Latin sessions during which she worked on samba and mambo. Vocally she had prepared a ballad and an uptempo from *West Side Story*.

The results were that her legs felt like mush and she couldn't remember a word of the songs.

Everyone was headed for the theater, which loomed over them like an alien spaceship—an enormous circular structure with a solid dome supported by thick pillars. Its walls were made of striped canvas tent material, hanging from the dome and hooked to the pillars. A long, wide tented corridor led to the theater entrance. It served as a kind of lobby, festooned with photos of past Playhouse shows. From inside the theater, Brianna could hear hammering, buzz saws, drills, recorded music. She checked her watch—9:47, thirteen minutes early—before poking her head through the entrance.

Her eyes adjusted quickly to the darkness. She had been in here a hundred times, back when her mom would take her to the plays, but the sight of it empty always took her breath away. Thick wood beams arched overhead, supporting the interior of the dome. Spotlights, hung from the beams, were trained on the stage below—it was like an island surrounded by seats. There were more than two thousand of those seats (if Brianna remembered right), on an angled cement floor that sloped downward to the stage. Behind the last row was a corridor that circled the theater. You got to your seats via six sloping cement ramps, aisles that separated the seats into sections like spokes on a wheel. Because there was no backstage, the actors had to use those ramps for their entrances and exits.

The stage below was the only brightly lit area, a circle covered with sound-absorbent black paint and little flecks of fluorescent tape left over from last year's shows. On it, a dozen or so people in shorts and T-shirts were constructing what looked like a drugstore counter, while a man in a tight-fitting Danskin outfit was trying out jazz-dance kicks and chassés to the music.

"Oh my god, this is the real thing," said Reese in a hushed tone.

"Can I help you?" came a voice from her right.

Brianna looked over. In the semidarkness she spotted a group of auditioners sitting quietly in the last row of seats.

A guy was heading toward her, clutching a clipboard. It wasn't until he came right up close that she recognized him. Although his hair was hanging loose instead of in a ponytail, the sharp nose and utter lack of a smile were unmistakable.

"Nantucket bay scallops, wrapped in bacon," Brianna said.

The guy nodded. "Daughter of the board member."

"We're here to audition," Brianna said. "We're on your list. I'm Brianna Glaser. But I guess you know that. And this is Reese Van Cleve and that's Harrison Michaels. Also, Charles Scopetta and Casey Chang, who will be seeing Mr. Little."

He eyed the clipboard. "Nope. None of those names are here."

"Really?" Brianna said, trying to peer at the clipboard. "Well, we were told by Mr. Bishop—"

"*I* was told by Mr. Bishop to be strict about the list," the guy said with a shrug. "Sorry. I've got a lot of people waiting."

As he walked toward the waiting actors Harrison murmured, "He's lying. Mr. Bishop wrote our names down!"

"On a business card," Charles reminded him. "And given his condition at the party, the card is probably in the bartender's wallet."

"Stay here, all of you," Brianna said, heading in the opposite direction, around the back corridor toward the other end of the theater. "I'll take care of this."

One of the many benefits of being the daughter of Evangeline Rogere-Glaser was that you knew how to get things done. And it wasn't by asking around at the bottom of the ladder.

"Excuse me?" Ponytail Undone's voice rang out. "Yo! *Where are you going?*"

He was jogging after her now, looking annoyed, the clipboard tucked under his arm.

"I told you," she said over her shoulder. "Ms. Richards is expecting—"

"Look, Ms. Richards says she's not to be disturbed. She's in meetings."

"But this is a mistake, that's all. I just want to—"

"E-mail her. Text her. Whatever. But I have a job, and I want to hold on to it."

"They're not going to fire you—you're a volunteer!"

"Yeah? Are you going to guarantee that? It's your mom who's the boss, not you."

Brianna spun around. The little dictator was glowering at her. He was cute, in a cocky, scraggly-bearded surfer-boy way. Probably used to getting whatever he wanted. This conflict was really a no-brainer. She wasn't pulling rank, just smoothing out a misunderstanding. But he wasn't seeing that. To his type, it was all about power. Nothing else. Brianna could smell that a mile away.

"What's your name, anyway?" she asked.

"Why do you want to know?"

From her pocket, Brianna whipped out a list of the theater personnel, which she had copied from her mom's files. "Let's see . . . interns . . . Trevor Eliades? Elton Scalsy? Reginald Stephens Heller?"

He winced. "Steve, okay? Not Reginald. Steve. Look,

you're right, I'm a volunteer. Which means I don't get paid for arguing with you while I have about thirty people waiting for me. So do me a favor and get your—"

"Is there a problem, Reginald?" a voice sounded from just inside the entrance.

A familiar tall, dapper man was walking toward them. He had thick black hair, gray on the sides, and was dressed in a seersucker jacket, an open white polo shirt tucked into reddish pants, and deck shoes with no socks. With his long neck and large blue eyes, his face seemed set in a look of perpetual surprise.

"Hey, Mr. Little," Steve replied. "We have some crashers here—"

The man walked right past Steve and took Brianna's hand, bowing. "Well, we-e-e-ll, little Brianna! So good to see you. Is your dear materfamilias here?"

"Mom's at work," Brianna said. "My friends and I just arrived to—"

"Indeed, indeed, to help around the theater," Mr. Little replied. "We spoke of that at the grand fete, didn't we? Refresh my memory . . . ?"

"Mr. Bishop said that three of us could audition," Brianna said. "And that you would try to find some backstage work for the other two."

"Ah, yes . . ." Even when he was frowning, Mr. Little looked slightly amused, as if he had just spotted a mildly fascinating insect. "Yes, I do recall something—oh, these parties do jam the circuitry, don't they? Well, *of course* I will honor whatever Stuart said. We must please our resident genius. So. Reginald, you will give the young thespians their audition slots—and the other two, come with me and I'll introduce you to Carol Richards, our stage manager."

"Thanks, Mr. Little," Brianna said.

"Not at all," he replied with a chuckle. "Welcome aboard! The next generation of Glasers, *et compagnie*—how exciting! Come along. *Vite! Vite!*"

As Mr. Little walked briskly along the corridor, Casey scurried behind. Charles gave a little hop and a barely audible squeal, blowing a kiss to Brianna.

"It's *Steve*," grumbled Reginald-who-was-called-Steve, taking a pencil from behind his ear. "Okay, I'll pencil you three in at the end."

As Steve begrudgingly wrote, Brianna eyed the crowd of beautiful people gathered near the theater door, waiting. She felt her heart pounding. She was one of them now. Along with Harrison and Reese. Who were both scrambling for seats.

And looking as nervous—and as too young—as she felt.

They were stunning, Reese thought.

Every one of them could have been a star. One after the other, the actors belted out Broadway tunes—with voices that nailed high notes like opera stars. The guys were gorgeous, the girls had legs a mile long, their turns were crisp, their leaps high, their landings soft and accurate. Pros. Total pros.

From her seat in the rear of the theater, she could see the silhouette of the back of Mr. Bishop's head, along with a few other bigwigs sitting together up front—most likely including the music director and choreographer, she guessed. Occasionally, after a good audition, Mr. Bishop would look up toward the actor and banter about his or her experiences.

Opened in a tour of *A Chorus Line* . . .

Four years with a tour of *Phantom of the Opera* . . .

Two seasons of summer stock on Cape Cod . . .

Graduated Juilliard last month . . .

Member of the New York City Ballet corps . . .

Alvin Ailey . . . Martha Graham . . . on vacation from the Yale Drama School . . .

What were they doing *here?* Reese wondered.

Right now a soprano was blasting the song "Tonight" as the piano accompanist pounded out powerful chords.

Reese turned to Harrison. "That was like a high Z," she whispered.

"The scale only goes up to G," Harrison said softly, "then goes back to A. That was probably a high C."

"Whatever it is, it would *kill* me," Reese admitted. "What are we doing here with these people?"

"It's not about them," Brianna said. "It's about you."

"What does *that* mean?" Reese said.

"Just stay inside yourself," Harrison advised. "Visualize yourself succeeding."

"I've been trying that for years—with you," Reese grumbled. "It doesn't work."

At the sound of Mr. Bishop's voice, the song stopped: "Okay, Sharon, thank you!"

"*And he rejected her!*" Reese whispered.

"Maybe he doesn't need her type," Harrison said. "She's blond and kind of old."

"He's hardly called back anybody," Reese pointed out. This was depressing.

She watched the soprano walk off the stage, head held high, wearing the same pleasant smile she'd had coming in. Actor after actor had done the same thing—maybe one out of ten had been called back. Reese knew that if that were her, she would be crying. Screaming. Was that what being an actor was like? You swallowed your pride, bottled up all your hurt? Or did you harden yourself to it? *How could you possibly do that?*

"Glaser?" Mr. Bishop called out.

"Eep," Brianna squeaked.

"Go for it," Harrison said.

"Stay inside yourself," Reese said.

"Thanks a lot, both of you," Brianna drawled.

Reese gave her a squeeze. "Break a leg. You'll be great."

Brianna pulled herself to full height. As she ran on stage, Reese grabbed Harrison's hand. They held on to each other tightly while Brianna gave her music to the accompanist and began singing "I Feel Pretty." Reese loved the song. She wished she could sing it. It belonged to the show's leading female character, Maria. She was a Puerto Rican immigrant—Reese could do the accent fine—and she was supposed to be mad in love with a Polish-American boy (Tony) from the rival gang. Reese could do the love part, too.

It was the notes—*high* notes—that would always do her in. Brianna was much more of a soprano.

"Oh my God, she's flat," Harrison whispered.

She wasn't five bars into it when Mr. Bishop called out, "Can you sing a ballad from the show?"

Brianna looked rattled—which, for her, meant slightly less than totally cocky. Smiling, she said, "How about 'One Hand, One Heart'?"

"Got it," said the accompanist, immediately playing the opening bars.

Brianna missed her entrance and had to start over.

"That's all right, sweetheart," Mr. Bishop said. "Happens to us all. Take it from the top, Fred."

The accompanist nodded and began again. But Brianna's confidence had been shaken. Reese could tell. The song was full of long, sustained notes, and Fred the accompanist played at a slow tempo—so Brianna ran out of breath twice.

A few bars into the song, Mr. Bishop cut Brianna off, and the choreographer hopped onstage. He gave Brianna a short Latin-style dance segment, which she performed while Fred pounded out "America." Reese had to shut her eyes. Brianna wasn't bad, just very . . . white. There was a way to do this, a way to make your hips more fluid, looser, sexier.

"Thank you!" Mr. Bishop called out immediately afterward. "Would you hold on a minute, dear?"

Reese was dying. The words *thank you*, she was learning, were the kiss of death. Generally they meant *no thank you.*

Mr. Bishop and his colleagues murmured to one another while Brianna stood there, looking uncertain. Finally he looked back up to her and said, "Can you stay?"

Brianna's face lit up. "Sure."

He liked her. She was in!

"*She made it!*" Reese squealed, wrapping her arms around Harrison.

"To the callbacks," Harrison reminded her. "It's not—"

"Van Cleve?" Mr. Bishop called out.

Thump.

Reese's heart nearly jumped out of her body. She tried to answer, but no sound came out of her mouth. "She's here," Harrison called out.

As Reese sidestepped along the row of seats and into the aisle, she banged her knee on an armrest, muttering a curse under her breath.

Mr. Bishop turned. "Are you all right?"

Reese fixed on his eyes. This was it. She knew from Drama Club experience that first impressions were crucial. This was where he either saw her as a Shark girl or not. "*Sí*," she said with a sexy smile, "*muy bien.*"

"Ah, *bueno*, señorita," Mr. Bishop replied with a bow and a sly smile.

Ha.

Brianna, still standing in the aisle, was staring in disbelief. Reese winked at her. A sometimes-I-have-good-ideas-too wink.

She stepped onto the stage, the pain in her knee magically gone. The vastness of this theater, the idea that you performed *in the round*, with people on all sides—not a traditional, long, "proscenium" stage like RHS—made her whole body feel light.

She handed Fred her music, nodding to him in such a way that a lock of hair fell across her face. He was a bright-eyed guy with a shaved head, multiple earrings, and a friendly face, and he grinned back.

Reese mounted the stairs deliberately, letting her hips sway from side to side. With each step, she felt more and more at home. She could feel the eyes on her, the impressions percolating. It was so familiar. When she turned to face the audience, the last hints of fear lifted. She took Mr. Bishop's smile and mirrored it back to him tenfold. The spotlight was warm like the beach sun, and the darkness of the surrounding seats seemed to enfold and comfort her.

She would sing as long as they wanted, and when they asked her to dance, she would set fire to the stage.

The opening chords of "A Boy Like That" rang out, and she began . . .

3

"WAS THAT REESE?" CHARLES CALLED OUT.

Casey scurried away from the tent flap opening. "Yes. Wasn't she *awesome*?"

Charles was sitting on a bench behind the theater and fanning himself with an old program. "I hope I live long enough to congratulate her before I die. I don't do well in the heat."

Casey nodded. It didn't feel too bad to her, temperature-wise, but she was a little nervous and scared. After a short meeting with Mr. Little, he had asked them to "relax" on the bench outside his office while he paged Carol Richards, the stage manager.

Mr. Little's office was in a small shingled hut, one of two buildings that sat behind the theater, separated from it by a grassy lawn and a walkway. The other building was a sprawling cinderblock bunker with multiple entrances, painted with blue and white stripes to match the theater. This contained the dressing rooms—two big ones for the girls' and boys' ensembles, and a small private one for the star—plus the costume area, props room, lighting shed, and a Green Room that doubled as a music rehearsal studio. All the doors were open. Ms. Richards was supposed to be in one of the rooms.

Carpenters and lighting people were walking purposefully in and out, grabbing equipment, conferring with one another, joking, calling out to the interns. The Sandy Shores kids were working hard, taking stuff across the walkway, in and out of the theater, running to follow directions. They were painting flats that were propped up against sections of the building wall. An older guy in olive khakis bustled around with a mop and bucket. He was pasty-faced and skinny with hair tied back in a ponytail, and he gave them a quick salute as he passed.

Charles's foot tapped impatiently. He looked at his watch for the hundredth time. "Let's find her."

"We're not supposed to," Casey reminded him. "She's supposed to find us, remember?"

Charles exhaled. He crossed his legs right to left, then left to right. "Did you ever see *Waiting for Godot?*" he asked. "It's about these two old guys. The plot is, they wait."

"That's all?" Casey said.

"Maybe that's what we're doing. It's a secret audition. They're recording us. Wouldn't that be fabulous? I adore Beckett."

An audible *pfffff*—someone's barely stifled laugh—sounded from Casey's left. A couple of intern painters were huddled together, their shoulders shaking, casting furtive glances at Charles and Casey.

"Glad we're so entertaining," Charles snapped. "I do a great Céline Dion too . . ."

As he rose from the bench, striking a pose with an imaginary microphone, Casey pulled him back. "*Charles!*" she scolded, then turned to the giggling interns. "Um, do any of you know where Carol Richards is?"

"Hey, I know you," said one of them—the curly-haired girl at the party who had introduced herself as the waitress from Rags.

"Oh. Hi," Casey said. "I'm Casey."

"Callie," the girl replied. "And that's Amber," she said, nodding to a girl whose long red hair was arranged in a French braid. "Are you two applying for internships?"

"You know there's a residency thing, don't you?" Amber said. "You have to live in Sandy Shores."

"Well, some of us are inside auditioning," Charles said. "But Casey and I shun the limelight."

"Auditioning?" Callie looked shocked. "Wait. They only use professional actors. Aren't you guys in high school?"

Charles nodded. "Can you believe it?" he said brightly. "Lucky dogs. It helps when one of your friend's moms runs the theater."

Casey elbowed him.

"My mom bakes cookies for opening night," said the red-haired girl. "Can I audition?"

"Maybe if you asked Mr. Little—" Casey said weakly.

"That was a joke," Callie said, her face darkening as she began painting again. "They tell us every year we can't audition. But they say if we volunteer to do this stuff—which I hate—they'll give us special preference when we're older."

"I like painting," Amber said with a shrug.

"And being ignored by the actors for a whole summer," murmured another of the interns, "unless something goes wrong."

Amber laughed. "And then they yell at you!"

Charles immediately took Casey's hand and began heading for the big cinderblock building. "Toodles," he called over his shoulder. "We're going to find Carol Richards."

"Do you know where we're going?" Casey whispered as she followed along.

"Let's start with the Green Room," Charles murmured. "Anything to get away from them before they start playing paintball with us. I don't cope well with other people's jealousy."

They approached a door at the far end of the building, which opened into a large, well-lit room with dusty wood-plank floors. A small team of interns was assembling lights, replacing colored gels, tinkering with machinery. In a corner, a girl and a guy sat sewing and chatting, next to a table piled high with costumes.

"Hi," Charles said, walking toward the table. "We're looking for Carol?"

"*Ms. Richards*," the girl said through a long curtain of

thin, shiny brown hair, "hasn't been feeling well. Maybe she went home."

The guy, whose misshapen hair and thick glasses gave him a Napoleon Dynamite vibe, grinned at them. "Yo, you're the Ridgeport people, right? Is it true you guys put on musicals that cost a million dollars?"

"No!" Casey replied.

"Yo . . . *Marc!*" the girl called across the room. "Have you seen Ms. Richards? These two want to see her. They're from Ridgeport."

One of the lighting interns turned and shrugged. But the man next to him, a stocky guy with dark features and a chiseled face, dropped his tools and came toward them, smiling. "Hey, there. I'm Lazlo Fibich, the lighting designer. This is Marc Schwartz, who's helping me this summer—and Lauren and Trevor, who work on costumes. We're sharing space because the costume room had sustained some water damage in the off-season. Good to have you aboard. I'll take you to Carol. Come."

Casey couldn't help noticing that no one said good-bye as they left.

"Are you interning?" Lazlo said as he led them out the door.

"We hope so," Charles replied. "It seems like a pretty close group, though. We're kind of outsiders."

Lazlo chuckled. "They'll warm up to you. You know, between the two towns there's this . . . rivalry."

They were now heading into one of the big dressing rooms through the back door, past a set of shower stalls. A long, platformlike table was bolted along the full length of the two walls that led toward the door. A chair and mirror marked each "place" for ensemble members, each mirror framed by a rectangle of bare lightbulbs. Clothing racks were all around—a long one divided the room and a couple more stood at the back. At one of the seats sat the choreographer they had seen earlier inside the theater.

Sitting next to him was a woman, leaning over several sheets of paper spread out over the long counter that ran under the mirrors. She was wearing half-glasses on a cloth lanyard that looped around her neck. When she looked up, Casey could see that she was very, very pregnant.

"Casey and Charles, this is Carol Richards," said Lazlo.

"Well. I am partial to people whose names begin with *C*," said Ms. Richards, extending an elegant, bracelet-jangling hand. She had short blond hair, a squarish jaw, and luminous blue eyes. "I'm just working out a rehearsal schedule with our choreographer."

"George Bunt," the man said, throwing them a hundred-watt Cheshire-cat grin. "She tolerates *G*s, too."

"Sorry to interrupt," Casey said. "Mr. Little said he would tell you we were here?"

Ms. Richards looked puzzled, then sighed and whipped out a cell phone. "Honestly, I love him dearly, but that man's attention span is somewhere between short and nonexistent."

Casey smiled. As Lazlo exited back to the Green Room, Ms. Richards jokingly scolded Mr. Little over the cell. After a quick conversation, she hung up and eyed them over the rims of her half-glasses. "Friends of the Glasers, eh? What can you do?"

Charles grinned. "The costumes, the scenery, the makeup, the props!"

"That's from 'There's No Business Like Show Business,'" Ms. Richards said with a chuckle. "So you're a jack of all trades. Hope you don't have allergies. The costume shop leaked over the winter, we lost half our costumes and the rest are at the cleaners, and there's mold all over the place. And how about you, Casey?"

"I, um, stage manage," she said.

"So you want to take my job in a bloodless coup?"

"No!" Casey said quickly. "I didn't mean that! I just—"

Ms. Richards burst out laughing. "Just kidding, dear." She gave Mr. Bunt a long, cryptic look. "Hmm. I thought we were at our limit with interns."

Mr. Bunt shrugged, and paged through a stapled-together sheaf of papers. "I think you may be right . . ."

Casey looked at Charles, worried that her nervously pumping heart showed beneath her polo shirt.

Ms. Richards rose from her seat slowly, fixing her gaze first on Charles, and then on Casey. She lifted her hands and placed them both on the swollen upper curve of her belly. "But if either of you thinks I would *dream* of refusing extra help in this condition," she said, "you are out of your mind. Charles and Casey, welcome to the Sandy Shores Playhouse!"

4

"SLING?" CAME CHARLES'S VOICE OVER THE PHONE. "Reese, will you calm down? I just heard you tell me you were cast as a sling."

"*Swing!*" Reese shouted into the receiver. "I'm the *swing!*"

It was hard to talk on a cell phone when you were jeté-ing from your bed to the bedroom floor. But Reese couldn't help it. Good news made her dance. It also made her want to scream. Which meant there needed to be someone to scream to. And Charles was always the default screamee.

"I just talked to Stuart—Mr. Bishop! I am now Reese Van Cleve, *professional actress!*"

"Aaaaaaagh!" Charles screamed back. "Oh! My

heart. My little Reese, with her name in lights. 'And introducing . . . Dancerslut!' I'll be so proud. But what's a swing? It sounds too kinky for *West Side Story*."

"It's the person who covers everyone in the chorus," Reese said, landing on her mattress in a sitting position. "*Everyone*. That means whoever is sick, I go on!"

"That *is* kinky! You would be a very hot Bernardo, in my opinion . . ."

"It's *not* that kind of theater, Charles. There's a separate boy swing and girl swing. Do you see how amazingly cool this is? It means they think I'm versatile—I can play Jet girl *or* Shark girl—"

"That Anglo–Puerto Rican thing you do *so* well," Charles said.

"And it also means I have to learn all the different chorus parts. Which is really scary, but I don't care. *I am so happy!*"

"And, of course, this friskiness has nothing to do with the fact that you'll be onstage with Mr. Malibu."

"That's not the most important part."

"But you nonetheless thought it important enough to post the news on Shawnnolan.com three minutes ago?"

"You read that? *You knew about this?*"

"Honey, nothing gets by me."

"Arrrrggghhh, I hate you!" Reese flopped back onto her bed. Some surprise. "Well, that's a stupid site, anyway. The real fan site is Nolanfan.com."

"Just a sec . . ." Charles's keyboard was clattering furiously. "Oh. Those photos. I'm turning red."

"Have you heard from the King and Queen?" Reese asked.

"Brianna and Harrison? No. I figured you had. Did they get cast?"

"I don't know. Mr. Bishop and Mr. Bunt didn't tell us at the theater. They gave us individual phone calls."

"Uh-oh," Charles said. "Silence from La Glaser is never a good omen . . ."

Harrison dug his hands into the Tupperware container of baklava he had brought over to Brianna's. Across the living room, Brianna was curled up in an armchair, talking on her cell to Mr. Bishop.

His stomach was still doing flips. Good flips. He was *in*—a tiny part in the chorus, one of the Sharks. He hoped it was because of his talent, but if he had gotten the part because of his friendship with Brianna, that was okay, too.

It was kind of shocking that she hadn't heard yet—but if *he* was cast, they couldn't reject the daughter of Mrs. Glaser.

Maybe they saved the VIPs for last.

"Thank you, Mr. Bishop," Brianna said into the phone, pulling her feet up underneath her. "I really enjoyed auditioning . . ."

Harrison smiled, thinking about his own phone call. It had come in about a half hour ago, when he was busing Table Four at Kostas Korner. Technically he was not supposed to answer the cell phone while working. Technically he was not supposed to shout "YYEEEEAH!"

at the top of his lungs in the middle of the floor, so loud that poor old Mrs. Minsky dropped her weekly peach melba into the lap of her light green paisley summer dress. But being that his dad was Kostas, the owner, Harrison was not only excused, but Mrs. Minsky got a promise of free dinner for a week—and every adult in the place received a complimentary milk shake to celebrate the news.

Harrison licked his fingers and reached for another honey-drenched piece of pastry, and then . . .

It happened.

Again.

He caught a glimpse of Brianna, bare feet tucked under her legs, her hair reflecting the light through the window like a shifting river of fire. He pictured her reaching for a piece of baklava, devouring it, and then licking her fingers. They would lick their fingers together and then fall on the floor laughing. He would turn on his side and offer her his honey-drenched fingers, and she would lick them . . .

What are you thinking?

Stop!

This had become a bad habit. It was all because of that night during *Grease* rehearsals, when things got out of hand. Hooking up had felt both amazing and amazingly weird, considering he and Brianna had been best pals since they were kids. For a while they'd gone through the usual stages: (1) Not Talking About It, (2) Brianna Complaining About Harrison Not Talking About It, (3) Sort-of Talking About It, and (4) Forgetting About It. Which was fine with Harrison.

They were friends. That was that. If you shut up about it, things shifted back. Sometimes when you talked too much, your problems just got bigger.

He surveyed the Glaser living room for new items—the green felt hat on George the stuffed peccary, a collection of Russian nesting dolls painted to look like the president and his advisers, a black Yale chair with gold trim. There was never any shortage of *stuff* here. Brianna's house was like a tent sale for insane rich people.

"Right . . ." Brianna was saying. "Sure . . . of course, I know exactly what you mean. Mm-hmm . . . that's how we run the Drama Club, too. Right. I understand. Thanks very much . . . yup, see you tomorrow!"

As she flipped the phone shut, Harrison dropped to his knees. *"Te adoro, Maria."*

"That's Tony's line," Brianna said. "You're not playing Tony."

"My role, Juano, is key," Harrison said. "How many Sharks are there—ten? He's tenth in succession to Tony. Who are you playing? Let me guess. They decided to fire the lead. You're Maria."

Brianna shook her head and sighed. "Mr. Bishop said I was very talented, but I wasn't exactly right for what he had in mind."

"Uh-huh. Don't string Juano along, he doesn't like it."

She shrugged. "Harrison, my audition sucked. He was honest, but very nice about it. He explained that my mom had called him and insisted that he not give us any special treatment—that we were to be seen just as he would see any other actor. So he honored that. I told him I understood."

"Wait—you're serious?"

"Yes."

"But you seem so—"

"Calm?" Brianna took Harrison's hand. "Remember what I said after *Grease*? About changing my life? I was serious then and I'm serious now. No more stressbaby for me. I am not going to freak out because I didn't get a part. Besides, Mr. Bishop says I can come by and talk to Carol Richards about working as one of her assistants."

"You would do that?" Harrison asked. "You would work with that guy Steve?"

"I liked stage-managing *Early Action*," Brianna said. "And Steve doesn't bother me."

Harrison held out the baklava. "Eat. You're scaring me, Brianna. This is not the old you."

"If you get any of this on the furniture and my mom makes me clean up," she said, "I will personally kick you where the sun don't shine."

"Now *that*," Harrison said with a smile, "is better."

5

"AND-A FIVE, SIX, SEVEN, *EIGHT!*" SHOUTED MR. BUNT.

He struck a pose, shoulders hunched, arms flexed, knees bent as Fred, the accompanist, began playing the song "Cool."

Mr. Bunt had a bit of a potbelly, but his movements were tough and pantherlike. He kept his body low and his steps into the floor—no bounce.

Reese was mesmerized. Her jazz dance teacher, Ms. Condos, was sharp and sleek, all Bob Fosse angles and jazz hands. But this guy was like an animal. He was pure sex.

"That's it, just up to measure twenty-three," he said to Fred, cutting him off. "Okay, kids, that's the idea. All of you, ensemble and leads—the feeling should be BAM! Powder keg! Like you can barely keep a lid on it. This is the fifties, and the world was just waiting to explode . . ."

Reese tried to pay attention to the history lesson, but Mr. Bunt's arms were distracting. They were like great outcroppings of granite, with veins running through them that rippled, disappeared, and then popped again as he moved.

"Gene Kelly," whispered Harrison, who was sitting next to her.

Reese nodded. It was a good comparison. "But twice as hot," she added.

"He's old enough to be your father," Harrison replied, "and probably gay."

Reese smacked him.

"Sensational, George!" Mr. Bishop called out as he shambled onto the stage, his graying beard, slumped shoulders, and stringy hair jolting Reese back into reality. "Sorry I'm a bit late, but I want to welcome my ensemble for the first day of rehearsals!"

Harrison clapped loudly as if it were a competition.

"Those of you who have been here before know the drill," he said. "We rehearse all day, with breaks, for two weeks. Some of you are here for the whole summer, but some are going to be with us for only one show."

"Right," Harrison said.

Mr. Bishop glanced at him curiously over his half-glasses, then went on to explain the rest of the season to the others—the pros who were staying all summer. Reese envied them. But it did seem like an impossible amount of work, performing one show by night and rehearsing the next show by day. "We are on a tight schedule for *West Side Story*," he went on. "Some scenes we will block only once and that's it. Remember, this is theater-in-the-round—no backstage. When you leave the stage during the show, you go up the aisles and then outside, preferably into the dressing rooms. If you need to, and you're very quiet, you can watch from the corridor behind the last row. You must learn not only the lines, the choreography, and the blocking, but also from which aisle to enter and exit. You will leave this summer not only in the best physical shape of your life but with twenty points added to your IQ."

Harrison laughed a little too heartily.

"You will have dance rehearsals with Mr. Bunt and musical rehearsals with Mr. Fredericks," Mr. Bishop continued. "He will insist that you call him Fred, but don't be fooled, he's really a sadistic hard-ass."

Fred immediately began playing an ominous theme on the piano with crashing chords—with a beaming, doughboy smile.

Harrison chuckled knowingly.

"Harrison, stop it!" Reese hissed.

"Normally our leads arrive at the theater only after the ensemble has rehearsed a few days," Mr. Bishop continued, "but as you all know, Mr. Nolan is already present, mainly because he's young and doesn't know any better."

"Yee-hah!" called out Shawn from the back of the theater.

At once, all the actors broke into applause. Shawn stood up halfway and nodded.

"He's blushing," Reese said.

"He has a sunburn," Harrison remarked. "And you don't mind when *he* calls things out."

"He can do whatever he wants."

"Excuse me while I vomit."

"Harrison, you are so transparent."

Brianna had been the first to arrive in the Green Room, but no one had sat next to her. The Sandy Shores kids were having a grand old time, joking and giggling among themselves. She looked at the clock, waiting for Ms. Richards to arrive at the meeting of the first-year interns: 10:02.

"And-a five, six, seven, *eight* . . . !"

Her stomach clenched at the sound that wafted in from the theater. The insistent tinkling of the rehearsal piano. The thumping of the choreographer's feet on the stage. They were beginning rehearsals already. With Harrison and Reese.

Without her.

Brianna closed her eyes and took a deep breath. *Stop it. No more stressbaby.*

She would have to present *positive* to Ms. Richards. Attend the meeting, then get her alone and ask her if she needed another assistant.

"Sorryyyyyy!" sang Ms. Richards as she bustled through the door. Her voice was like a show tune. Casey rushed in behind her, beaming from ear to ear as she sat in the empty seat next to Brianna.

Brianna squeezed Casey's hand. "You look happy," Brianna whispered.

Casey squeezed back and stared admiringly at Ms. Richards, who began speaking a mile a minute.

"Don't get used to this, kids," she said. "I am never ever late and I expect you to match that. So, first of all, a big

summer welcome to all the first-year interns from me"—
she patted her protuberant belly—"and Orson."

The Sandy Shores interns all cracked up. Brianna
turned to Casey, who shrugged.

"This is going to be the Playhouse's best summer ever,"
Ms. Richards went on. "I've heard Shawn—our Tony—
sing, and he is magnificent. We have a generous budget,
and some extraordinary plans. The more the merrier, and
I'm expecting that *all* of you will be professional caliber
within a week or so. With Orson on the way, I will be
needing tremendous help, so I now have not one, but two
wonderful assistant stage managers. Most of you already
know Steve, who was here last year. But I'd like to also
introduce Casey Chang. Let's give it up for Casey!"

Brianna's jaw dropped. *Casey* was going to be an ASM?
So it wouldn't only be Steve the Creep. Working with
Casey—*that* would be fun.

Casey gave a modest wave to the room.

"Now, we have a lot to go over before we get started,"
Ms. Richards said, drawing a stack of papers from her bag.
"Papers to sign, departments to assign. You will be working
in either costumes, props, stage crew, or sets. As soon as
we mount our first production, we begin immediately
working on the next . . ."

As she went on, Brianna took notes. Summer stock was
going to be intense. Her head was spinning by the time
Ms. Richards wrapped up at ten forty-five. As the interns
all lined up for their assignments, Brianna waited with
Casey at the end of the line.

Ms. Richards greeted her with a huge smile. "Hi,

Brianna," she said. "I remember you from when your mom brought you here as a girl—how long ago . . . ?"

"When I was nine, I think," Brianna said guiltily.

"Mr. Bishop told me you gave a wonderful audition, and he wished he could have expanded the number of Jets girls."

"Thanks," Brianna said. "I'm happy just to be working here. He told me you might need another assistant. I stage-managed our last show at RHS."

"She was an amazing SM," Casey added.

"Really?" Ms. Richards replied. "Thank goodness. Sometimes the serious actors don't deign to do backstage work."

"I love it," Brianna said decisively.

"Fabulous," Ms. Richards said. "I could use someone strong and decisive on stage crew."

Stage crew?

Creeping around during blackouts? Picking up props off the stage, dressed in grubby black clothes? Going home covered in dust and other people's sweat?

"Well, I've never really done that—"

"Slow set changes will kill a show's rhythm," Ms. Richards said. "A good stage crew is worth its weight in gold."

"Um, actually, I was hoping I could be another ASM."

"Where is she?" a voice barked from just outside the door. Steve shuffled into the room as if he badly needed a cup of coffee. "Casey. Come on. The rehearsal began."

As Casey left with him, Ms. Richards sighed. "It's tempting, Brianna, but honestly, I'm all set for ASMs. I'm afraid there wouldn't be enough for you to do and you'd be bored. I suppose you could talk to Casey and switch. But I wouldn't discount being the head of stage crew. It's an important position. I think you would be happier."

Brianna could feel the eyes of some of the interns on her. Already they resented the Ridgeport kids. The last thing she wanted to do was argue. This was all about being a team player. "Okay," she said. "Sounds great."

Ms. Richards beamed at her. "You'll see, this will be fun. Mr. Sainte is our set designer, and he's just about finished with the plans. The one who looks like Matthew Fox. Between you and me—and *not* my husband—he is a total dreamboat. Hottie. Whatever you kids call that. Anyway, he's been working with Steve, who has the list of set changes so far. So first thing, you can get that list and we'll take it from there. Meanwhile, if you have some time, feel free to drop in on the other departments. Summer stock is an amazing learning experience."

Brianna smiled. "Thanks, I will."

As Ms. Richards took a call on her walkie-talkie, Brianna wandered outside. The air seemed to have warmed about ten degrees. She let the sun hit her face, trying to sort everything out. The sweet musty smell of wisteria breezed past, and the jazzy chords of the song "Cool" rang out from the theater. All around her, people were bustling from the theater to the various rooms in the outbuilding. A peal of laughter came from Mr. Little's office.

She wanted to make this work. It was theater. Real theater. Professionals. People with Broadway experience. Not summer camp where Janie Milliken would switch a costume just for spite, or Spenser Parker would sing every song a quarter tone flat. As she stepped into the theater, a rush of cool air greeted her. To her left, Steve was talking to a group of interns, including Casey.

She waited until he looked her way. "I'm supposed to get the list of set changes," she explained. "For the stage crew."

"Set changes," he repeated in an annoyed, condescending voice, as if she had just farted in his face. "Well, it's too early for *that*. Sorry."

What a turd. "Oh," Brianna said flatly. "I guess I'll tell Ms. Richards that you weren't ready."

He looked at her curiously. "I thought you were going to act in the show."

"I wasn't cast. So I'm helping backstage. If that's all right with you."

Steve glanced at the clipboard in his hand and said, "If you really want to help, start in the ladies' room. The supplies are in the small closet in back of the Green Room. You have to walk around the building—"

"Are you serious—you want me to clean the toilet?" Brianna said.

"Dan is doing the men's," Steve said. "I could have him double up, if that's too far beneath you."

"Whoa. Wait," Brianna said. She could not believe this. No one talked to her like this. Especially in front of other people. "I don't work for *you*. I work for a real person. Ms. Richards."

Turning on her heel, she left. This was not fun. Theater was supposed to be fun. Working at the Krok Fund with

Excel spreadsheets would be more stimulating than hanging with Steve.

Obviously there wasn't enough for her to do. Which meant they wouldn't miss her if she left.

She barged across to the Green Room for her bag. It was hooked over the back of a chair. In the back of the room, a woman dressed and made up totally Goth dumped a pile of clothes on a table. "Let's work in here," she was saying to someone. "I can't stand that mildew smell in the costume room."

Brianna was about to go when she heard Charles's voice. "Ms. Gruber? Here's your problem, darlin'. These are too low." He was examining a pair of jeans, oblivious to Brianna, as other interns brought in more piles of clothes. "In the fifties, they wore these high-waisted things. Kind of like my grandfather. But it was cool then."

The Goth woman looked at the jeans and sighed. "Of course, but I have neither the time nor the budget. And call me Ariel, please."

"And this soft, light blue stressing?" Charles said with dismay. "Very twenty-first century. Everyone wore them dark blue and stiff. Leave it to me. My cousin works for this vintage clothing buyer in New York. I snap my fingers and voilà." Charles attempted snapping his finger but made no sound. "I never was good at that. Also, I've already started sketches on some ideas for the dance at the gym . . . Oh, hi, Bri! Can you snap your fingers?"

Before Brianna could reply, Ariel gave her a mournful look and slid out of the room.

An intern barged into the room, nearly colliding with Charles. "Uh, you're kind of in the way?"

"*Pardonnez-moi*, Lauren," Charles said, stepping out of her way as the girl barged by him with a pile of costumes. "I was telling Ms. Gruber about these fabulous sketches I made for the—"

"I know." The girl, whose hair was just short of a buzz cut, had a head that outlined a perfect question mark in profile. As she dumped the costumes on a table, she said, "Not sure how to say this, but, um, Ariel is the designer, okay? Not us."

"Zzzzip," Charles said, pretending to zip his lips. Suddenly he grasped a thick brocaded robe that had a huge stain. "Ohhhh, this has got to be from *The King and I*. What a tragedy!"

"We're not supposed to handle the damaged stuff!" Lauren said, rubbing her forehead. "Look. Charles, we're kind of okay for help here in costumes. Maybe you can check lighting or sets or something. Or just . . . go away."

As Lauren stepped out of the room, Charles stood there slack-jawed. And that's when he finally noticed Brianna. "I did not hear that, did I?" he said.

"Nice bunch, huh?" Brianna remarked. "Welcoming."

"They hate us," Charles said.

"Guess we threaten their little kingdom," Brianna replied, slinging her bag over her shoulder.

"Where are you going?"

"I don't know. Far away from Nasty Shores Playhouse. The beach, maybe."

Charles thought a moment. Then he grabbed a shoulder bag from a chair. "I'll bring the sunscreen."

6

"A CRUISE WOULD BE NICE," CHARLES SAID, crunching a seashell underfoot. "You, me, selected friends, a yacht with a crew. I'll provide the decorations, you handle the entertainment. And every few moments, Ariel Gruber can come out from below and announce, 'Gloomy seas ahead!'"

The beach was a few degrees warmer than the theater. Brianna lifted her face to the sun and felt the heat through the early summer breeze. They were both fully dressed, having come straight from the theater, and she wished they had gone home first to get swimsuits. "The nastiness trickles down from the top," she said. "Steve. I think he poisons their minds."

"Exactly," Charles said, making a sudden move toward

a seagull, who screeched, hopped, and then settled back down. "He's a vampire. Have you ever seen him smile? No, because *that* would reveal the pointy canines."

"They think we're rich and lazy and overprivileged."

"Well, *you* are, darlin'. Which is why they hate you most of all. But the rest of us are not far behind. Lauren keeps a Charles Scopetta voodoo doll. Ouch. I felt a prick."

"But you're not paranoid."

"Never."

Brianna smiled. Charles always made her feel better. She gave him a squeeze, which nearly made him fall on the sand.

As they moved farther from the boardwalk and closer to the surf, the crashing of the waves grew louder and the vast expanse of yellow-white sand became a sparse neighborhood of umbrellas and blankets. Radios and portable players blasted music, and a loud game of volleyball raged near the lifeguard stand.

Over by the net, a chiseled arm waved at them, attached to a set of chiseled pecs and abs that served as a connector between the narrow waist and unbearably beautiful face of Kyle Taggart. "Dudes!" he called out.

He was running toward them now, accelerating. His hair, streaked golden by the sun, trailed behind him like a flag, his thickly muscled legs digging hard into the sand.

"Oh my God, he's going to run us over," Charles said.

"Kyle, don't," Brianna said. "Don't, Kyle—aggghhh!"

Without breaking stride, he lifted her, one arm behind her shoulder and the other behind her knees, spinning her around, bellowing like a conquering caveman. She felt the slipperiness of his sweat-glistened arms, the vague coconutty scent of sunscreen on his neck. His grip was strong and sure, and she screamed, letting her head fall back, looking up to the sky. The clouds swirled into a white-blue pudding—and for a moment she was seized with a feeling, a memory that made her feel dizzy and cold.

She'd been here before. *They'd* been here. Almost exactly a half year ago, in just about the same place. He had taken her in his arms then, too—spinning all the worry and tightness out of her. It felt the same, but it had been nighttime then, freezing cold, and Kyle had raced into the water, stark naked, daring her to follow.

There was something about Kyle's act—the freedom, that incredible "screw you" to the rest of the world . . . it was contagious, made you want it for yourself.

She was laughing by the time he set her down. "Kyle," she said, "you are a madman."

Kyle turned to Charles. "You're next."

"If you even try . . ." Charles said, hopping back.

"Joke!" Kyle said. He nodded toward the volleyball net. "Hey, we're losing a couple of players. Come join us."

"You go ahead, Bri," sputtered Charles, who hated sports. "I'm, uh, wearing shoes."

Brianna grabbed him by the hand. "Take them off!"

She ran toward the net, towing Charles, who protested the whole way. A squeal of hellos greeted them—Aisha Rashid and Ethan Smith from Drama Club, Pete Newman and Benny Eaton from the football team, Darci Feder from math class. As Brianna quickly kicked off her flip-flops, she saw Charles carefully removing his Vans, folding up his white ankle socks, and tucking them inside.

"Charles is on Aisha's team," Kyle said, preparing for a serve. "Brianna, you're with us."

He windmilled his arm and struck the ball. As Charles placed himself in front of the net, the ball sliced through the air on a line, directly at his face.

"Oh!" he cried out, shooting his arms forward for protection. The ball bounced off his hand and went straight in the air. Aisha and Pete jumped at the net, on opposite sides, but it was Aisha who spiked the ball for a point.

"Woo-hoo!" she cried, hugging Charles. "Great assist!"

"Thanks," Charles replied. "I'm, uh, an assister by nature."

"Let Charles serve," Aisha called out.

"Serve?" Charles said, catching the ball. He walked tentatively to the back, pushing up his glasses, which had slid down his nose. His black T-shirt and long black pants were already soaked as he turned, raised the ball over his head, and threw it.

"You have to punch it," Pete said, catching the ball.

"Just testing you," Charles replied.

Brianna buried her head in her hands.

By the end of the game, Brianna had completely forgotten about the Sandy Shores Playhouse. The score was 21–19 Kyle's team, or 21–18 Aisha's team, depending on which side you were on, so everyone was happy. The guy selling drinks and frozen candy had been by twice, and they had cleaned him out. Charles had actually gotten pretty good, making a couple of solid, sneaky hits. But he looked exhausted.

Carefully placing his glasses inside his shoes, he took a sip of bottled water, turned toward the ocean, and calmly said, "Last one in pays for lunch."

"We don't have swimsuits!" she replied.

"So? Clothes dry out."

Brianna had never seen him run so fast.

She sprinted after him along with the rest of the crowd, kicking up sand all around and then hitting the water with screams of shock. It was freezing, but it felt excellent. Kyle swam up next to Brianna and said, "Race you," quickly heading out to sea at top speed.

"Oh, right, that's fair!" Brianna propelled herself forward. Kyle had a strong stroke, and a good head start, but no one could beat Brianna's Camp Silver Glade crawl—even with a shirt and shorts on. She pulled even with him and then surged ahead.

But Kyle was powerful and kept pace with her until a piercing whistle made them both stop.

"COME IN IMMEDIATELY OR YOU WILL BE FINED!" a voice shouted over a bullhorn.

"Crap," Kyle said, treading water. "How are we going to know who won?"

"I did," Brianna said.

Kyle lunged and dunked her under. "Race you back."

The jerk. Brianna emerged, coughing out water. "That's cheating!" she cried out.

But he was in motion. Swimming and laughing at the same time. She took off at top speed, but he was too far ahead and too strong. He reached the shore first and took off at a run.

She chased him across the beach, keeping up with him as he zigzagged, until they finally collapsed, laughing, in the sand.

"Auggh, we're covered," Brianna said.

Kyle shrugged. "Guess we have to go back in again."

Some of the others were heading their way, including Charles, soaked in his black outfit—all of them giddy and laughing.

Brianna hadn't felt this good in days. *This* was what vacation was supposed to be. She smiled at Kyle and thought about next summer. They would have all gotten into colleges by then, would probably be working jobs, looking forward to the future. "I want this to be the greatest summer ever," she said.

He beamed. "Then it will be."

"Easy for you to say. I blew my audition,"

"Dude, that sucks. What about, like, doing sets and stuff?"

Brianna nodded. "I tried that. But all the Sandy Shores kids were total snots."

Kyle put his arm around her and gave a squeeze. "Hey, no surprise about that, right? I mean, if I was them and I wanted to be in the show? And they didn't let me, but they let these strange kids from another town audition?"

Brianna thought about it a moment. She hadn't really

looked at it from that perspective. He had a point. "Yeah," she said with a sigh. "I guess you're right. Maybe I should just quit."

"And do what, work for your mom in an office?" Kyle laughed.

"You think it's funny—"

"Yo, chill. Figuring out this problem isn't, like, rocket science."

"Really, Kyle? What's the answer?"

"Hey, you know the drill." Kyle shrugged. "You taught it to me. Just do what you love. Everything else follows."

Brianna smiled. He was a goon, but a smart goon.

And just like that, she realized exactly what she needed to do the next morning.

7

"NICE JOB, BOYS AND GIRLS!" MR. BUNT CALLED OUT, glancing at his watch. "We have a long way to go. Let's break for lunch. See you in an hour, and don't forget what we learned!"

Reese grabbed a towel from her shoulder bag and wiped her forehead. Her mind reeled from remembering all the dance combinations. Around her, the other dancers grumbled, laughed, bickered, asked one another questions. It had been an intense rehearsal. Mr. Bunt showed you everything only once—twice if you were lucky—and you were expected to know it right away.

It was another world from high school, even from RHS. Not only the speed, but the dancers themselves. They all walked with perfect turnout, their legs lean and muscle-toned. They did triple pirouettes on a dime, with unbelievable control of every part of their bodies. They all had gorgeous alignment and perfect balance. No one ever seemed to miss a step.

It was exhilarating.

A few of the dancers were jumping off the stage, reaching for their shoulder bags, but many of them remained on the stage. Reese could hear snippets of conversation:

"The way we did it in Milwaukee . . ."

"Is this the original choreography?"

". . . a double, not a triple pirouette . . ."

"Is it BA-ba—BA-ba-dap, or ba-BA—ba-BA-DAP?"

Reese hovered at the edges. That was her role in all of this—edge hovering. As the "swing," she had to hover in the background, somehow learning every dancer's steps, for the day when she might have to replace someone.

Reese smiled, said hi to the dancer nearest her, and got only the briefest nod in return. The steps weren't hard, really. It was the hovering. When you hovered, people didn't know what to do with you. You were there but you weren't.

Shawn was ambling down the ramp now. "You guys are *hot!*" his voice shouted in the darkness.

Reese froze up. He'd been watching. Which meant he had seen Reese, separate from the others, dancing by herself, like the odd girl out at the party. The unhot among hot. The hoverer.

Did he know what a swing was?

She jumped off the stage, to where her shoulder bag lay in the front row of seats. A few of the other dancers were wiping their faces with towels, gathering their bags for lunch. Nearest to Reese was a blonde with legs that seemed about a foot longer than normal, and blue eyes as big as platters. She smiled back, with a polite blank look as if she had never seen Reese before. Next to her, another dancer with jet-black hair and deep brown Winona Ryder eyes smiled also.

Reese figured someone would ask her to come out to lunch, but no one did. They just seemed bewildered by the fact that she existed.

As Reese reached for her bag, she spotted Shawn again. He had settled in the third row, his feet propped up on the seat in front of him. A script was open on his lap, and he was mouthing words to himself. As he read quietly, he made faces along with the lines, occasionally sipping from a water bottle.

Reese put down her bag. O-o-o-okay, why rush things? Might as well "warm down," she thought. Good dance technique was crucial. Especially when the view was so nice.

She did a couple of pliés then dropped into a half split on the floor in front of the first row of seats.

"Don't tell me that doesn't hurt," came Harrison's voice from behind her. He was walking toward her down the ramp.

"Oh—you're talking to me?" she said softly as he plopped down into a seat next to her. "That must mean I exist. For a minute I was having doubts."

"Doubts?" he said. "You?"

"Don't these people make you feel inferior?"

Harrison shrugged. "They make me feel inspired. They were probably like us a few years ago, and now look at them. Want to have lunch?"

Reese eyed Shawn, still buried in his script. "Um, I'll stay here a while. It's the first day of rehearsal. I need to get in shape."

"Uh-huh," Harrison said with a knowing glance. "If you change your mind, I'll be at the Chinese place across the street, eating a huge plate of shrimp chow fun, followed by some ginger ice cream."

"Bring me back a doggie bag."

"No way."

As Harrison left, Reese climbed up on the stage and tried to remember Mr. Bunt's choreography. The beginning of the number had a sudden, tricky rhythm that she didn't quite get . . . it was like *this* . . .

"Whoa, how did you do that?"

Hallelujah.

Shawn was leaning forward, arms on the seat in front of him, smiling at her.

His eyes were like torches on a foggy night. Her knees were like rubber bands. And her brain had to stop churning out romance-novel observations.

"You mean this?" Reese said, gathering herself. She placed her right hand on her lower torso and repeated the move she had been practicing—just a matter of shifting weight, moving her hips side to side. "It's actually pretty easy."

"That is so awesome," Shawn said. "Fluid with the hips . . . the way you dig into the floor . . . *I* can't do that."

"It's a Latino thing." Reese repeated the move, slowly. "Like this . . ."

Now he was scrambling down the aisle. Hopping onto the stage.

Reese felt a little bubble of freezing cold air jam her throat. And suddenly she was onstage with Shawn Nolan, and in a moment her whole life seemed to have changed, and she wanted a photographer, a filmmaker, a cardiologist to print out her heartbeat — anything to record the reality of this moment.

"Show me again?" he said.

"Um . . ." Reese swallowed. What did Tony do in this scene? "Wait. Tony enters later in the dance. He does something different. With Maria . . ."

"So?" Shawn shrugged. "I want to do this. It's fun."

Fun? He was doing this for *fun*?

He tried to imitate Reese's move himself and sucked pretty badly. Which was somehow comforting.

"Not bad," Reese lied, "for a white guy."

Shawn laughed. "Uh, you are, too."

"A white guy? No way."

She was joking with him. Teasing. It just came naturally. Were you supposed to tease stars? What if they were insulted? They were used to being around sophisticated big shots in Hollywood, not snotty high school slings.

Swings.

But he was smiling like a normal person, like some guy who liked to dance and who just happened to be outrageously gorgeous. So she held out her arms in a dance-partner pose, the way she would in a class.

As he came closer, Reese's breath quickened and she wondered if people could get heart attacks at age sixteen. His left hand touched her right and for a moment she saw an image from the movie *Dr. Zhivago*, where Julie Christie meets Omar Sharif in a trolley car and the camera cuts to the electrical wires at the top, when suddenly . . .

Zzzzzap!

Shawn's hand felt warm. His other arm, which was circling around her waist, was strong and confident, not scrawny and tentative like some of the guys in Ms. Condos's Saturday class.

He smiled at her and she clenched up. "P-p-p-put . . ."

"Yes?" Shawn said.

"Put your hand in the small of my back," Reese managed to say. "That's where all the movement starts from."

Shawn took her left hand and wrapped his right around her waist. "Like this?"

Reese concentrated hard. She knew how to do this. She rotated her hips, dipping to the floor and up again, pulling Shawn along.

He tried. He wasn't so bad. "Good," she said. "Now you lead, and I'll follow."

It took a few tries until he got the hang of it.

"We break away . . . *here*," Reese said on the beat, spinning away from him and kicking her leg into the air behind her, her hands lifting a phantom skirt.

Shawn watched and did a frenetic version of the same thing.

"HAAAAH!" Reese's hand flew to her mouth.

Shawn, who had kept a straight face, was losing it now.

He was cracking up—maybe at his own stupid move, maybe at her wack laugh. Whatever. It didn't matter. Their laughs were echoing through the theater.

"I know, I suck," he finally said.

"No!" Reese replied. "It was just that—no, you're good! You're going to do really well!"

Mr. Little appeared in the one of the rear tent flap exits, near his office. "Shawn? It's your agent? He said he's been trying your cell!"

Shawn whirled around, his hand reaching for his pants pocket. "Dang, it ran out of charge."

He leaped off the stage. As he ran up the ramp, he spun around to smile at Reese and call out, "Thanks!"

She took that smile and that word and held it close.

June 25, 06:42 P.M.
SCOPASCETIC: so. what did we miss?
dancerslut: omg omg omg charles he is so so so hot.
SCOPASCETIC: greek boy sez u and sn were nearly doin it to the mambo?
dancerslut: no! not true
dancerslut: well, yet. WHERE WERE U????? i coulda used a witness.
SCOPASCETIC: at the beach, cooling off. but la glaser & i have decided to return.
SCOPASCETIC: queue trumpets.
dancerslut: i think its cue. someone said u pitched some kind of hissy fit?
SCOPASCETIC: some kind. bri too. we were gonna

quit & spend the rest of the summer sur la plage.
but we had our reality check. we decided it would
be too boring
SCOPASCETIC: *despite my superior volleyball*
skills . . .
SCOPASCETIC: *so we're coming back & vowing to*
make ourselves useful somehow . . . somewhere . . .
somedaaaaaayyyyy
dancerslut: lol. there's a place for u.
SCOPASCETIC: *but mostly, of course, because the*
summer has quickly become JUICY thanks to you.
can't wait . . .
SCOPASCETIC has signed off.

Reese smiled and minimized the screen.

She stared at the Nolanfan.com home page festooned with photos of Shawn—as a baby, as a child star, on his first sitcom.

Quickly surfing the photo gallery, she found an image she had not yet seen. It was a little cheesy and pixelated— he was grinning in a very wholesome way on the cover of next month's *Teen*. But he was also bare-chested and really buff.

She gave a dreamy sigh. No one should be that gorgeous, not to mention insanely hot. But he was. And he had danced with *her*.

And that, she promised herself, was only the beginning.

8

MS. RICHARDS, I CAN'T BLAME YOU IF YOU'RE
*totally angry with Charles and me over our selfish act,
leaving yesterday's rehearsal without notice . . .*

Oh, God, too fake.

Brianna sped around the side of the theater, checking
her watch. Fifteen minutes till the start of rehearsal. She
hoped to reach Ms. Richards before the start of the day.
What was the best way to apologize? She wasn't used to
apologizing. She should have consulted Casey.

*Hey, Carol. Yeah, we suck. Soooo sorry. Charles and I
promised to get on our hands and knees and lick the corners
clean if we have to . . .*

Too casual?

"'Morning," a voice called from above. "Can I help you?"

The voice startled Brianna. She looked up to see a skinny, pasty-faced, middle-aged guy with a ponytail and bulging tool belt calling down to her from atop a ladder. He looked vaguely familiar. Under his overalls, he was wearing a *Godspell* T-shirt, which made her smile. "I'm Brianna Glaser, one of the interns. Just here to talk to Ms. Richards . . ."

"Dan Workman, the custodian—here to repair a rip," he said with a friendly salute. Brianna remembered that salute from the morning before. He was the guy who had been toting a mop around. He seemed friendly. At least someone here was.

"Ms. Richards is in the office," he went on, "talking with Mr. Little and a couple of the other interns. Go ahead in."

"Thanks," Brianna said. As she headed for the door, she recalled something from the day before.

Dan.

Steve had mentioned a Dan. When he ordered Brianna to clean the women's room. *Is that too far beneath you?* he had said. *Dan is doing the men's. I could have him double up.*

Dan was the janitor. The way Steve had said it, Dan sounded like the name of another intern. He had done that on purpose. To make Brianna feel guilty. To trick her into cleaning the toilet!

Before she could grip the doorknob, the door flew open.

"Oh! Sorry!" Charles said, bouncing out. "I just apologized to Ms. Richards. I was going to wait for you, but I got all tingly and excited, and I knew I had to *carpe* the *diem*. That means . . . oh, dear. Are you mad at me? You look mad. Was it the Latin?"

"Sorry, Charles." Brianna forced a smile. "I'm just distracted. I was dreaming of ways to torture Steve."

"Ah, good, I like positive thinking," Charles replied. "Well. To make a short story long, Carol is the bomb. I told her all about yesterday—in my own tactful, tasteful way, of course. She totally understood. She hinted the Sandy Shores kids are a little bent out of shape. They're aspiring thespians, too . . ."

Brianna sighed. "Yeah. I kind of figured that out."

"Anyway, she had a wonderful idea. You and I are going to float for the week—from department to department, asking who needs help. We'll meet people, show our talents and fabulous personalities. So I'm heading over to Lazlo Fibich in lighting—mainly because I love that name. My advice to you? Talk to Casey. She's in Mr. Little's office. Her position is equal to Steve's. Maybe you can collaborate with her. And even team up against Grumpy."

"Charles, I love you," Brianna said, giving him a squeeze.

Charles beamed. "I am all about love, and the relief of pain and suffering."

Turning toward the lighting shop, Charles nearly collided with an intern who had a track lighting rig on his shoulders.

"A lighting person, what luck!" Charles said. "Take me to Lazlo. I'm an intern—Charles Scopetta?"

"Marc," the guy grunted, looking a little baffled. Bafflement sat well with him, Brianna thought. With his curly brown hair, brooding eyes, and wiry runner's build, he looked like a textbook illustration of an ancient Roman warrior. He turned toward an open door in the cinderblock building. "Follow me."

Charles jogged after him, calling over his shoulder, "Say hi to Casey for me!"

Brianna backtracked to Mr. Little's office. The door opened to a small antechamber, where Casey was stuffing a clipboard into her shoulder bag. Ms. Richards, sitting next to her, was talking intently on the phone.

"Bri, I'm really glad you're here," Casey said, looking relieved. "Things are crazy because of the water damage in the costume shop. The shipping company is coming in early—today—with a huge load of rented costumes. I'm supposed to clear the scene shop to store the shipment. Ms. Richards says I can use you to help." As Brianna followed Casey out of the office, she continued breathlessly, "We're supposed to keep the clothes there for a day or two. The shop isn't used much during the first show of the season. A lot of the work is done directly on the stage." Casey glanced at Brianna tentatively. "Are you okay? I hear you got pretty mad. I tried to message you around one A.M.—"

"I went to bed early," Brianna replied. "Why were *you* up so late?"

Casey turned red. "Chip. He was telling me all about

his course assignments at Johns Hopkins. I wish I could visit him."

Brianna put her arm around Casey. The idea of anyone pining over nerdy Chip, the genius who'd written the Drama Club's spring play, was just too cute for words.

Hammering greeted them as they reached the scene shop. Inside, Brianna recognized Callie, the curly-haired waitress from the fund-raiser. She was trying to set a section of Cyclone fence, about waist-high with small wheels at the bottom, into some kind of track.

"Nice work," Brianna said.

"Thanks. It's a fence, for the rumble scene," Callie said. "When the Jets and Sharks finally have the big fight. They have to slide it open. So we're making a track."

"Kind of low for a fence," Brianna remarked, running her finger along the top.

"Um, it's theater in the round? The audience is on all sides, so you can't have any scenery that blocks people's view."

"Ms. Richards asked us to clear the shop," Casey said nervously. "Just temporarily. We're expecting a shipment of costumes."

"Oh . . ." Callie said, confused. "But there's plenty of room here if we *don't* move stuff. Can't you just work around us?"

Casey shrugged. "Sorry, I'm just doing what Ms. Richards said."

"You better not cross Casey," Brianna said with a pleasant smile. "There's no telling *what* she's capable of."

Callie narrowed her eyes. "Is that supposed to be a joke?"

"Yo, wassup in here?" Steve's voice called out from behind them.

"They're telling me to take this apart and evacuate the shop," Callie said over her shoulder, "to make room for costumes."

"Ms. Richards didn't say *evacuate*," Casey said. "Just clear the shop temporarily. It's a huge shipment."

Steve sighed. "I've worked here for two summers. We've been here before, we know how big the shipments are. We can handle it without clearing."

"But—" Brianna began.

"Look, do you want me to get Ms. Richards?" Steve interrupted. "Do you want me to bring her here? Because she's busy and pregnant. Our job is to make her life easier, not harder."

"Uh, wait, how did *following her instructions* get redefined as *making her life harder*?" Brianna said.

Casey stepped between them and gently guided Brianna outside the shop. "No problem. We'll make it work," she said.

As they walked into the sunlight, Brianna seethed. "Did you hear that son of a—"

"Shh," Casey said, linking arms. "Let's be friends with these people, Bri. Look, if Ms. Richards says anything, I'll just tell her what happened. Then, if Callie gets overwhelmed by the costumes, it'll be her own fault."

"Right. You're right," Brianna said. "Sensible."

Halfway to the office, they spotted Charles slumping

out of the theater. He nodded glumly toward them and said, "Am I charming? Tell me, you guys. Am I funny and fizzy and disarming and lovable?"

"Should I take those one at a time?" Brianna said.

"Assuming the answer is yes," Charles went on, "then why is everybody treating me like I stepped in dog poop?"

"You too?" Brianna said.

Casey laughed. "Guys, I think I see the laundry truck out front. I'll be back soon."

As she jogged away, Charles slumped on a bench. "Why did we bother coming back today, Bri?" he said. "They act like I have cooties. The harder I try, the worse it gets. I'm not sure I want to spend the whole summer like this."

A loud cackle came from inside the scene shop, behind them.

"It's 'cause of her mom, of course," a voice was saying. "They're like, stupid-rich. . . ."

Steve's voice.

Charles's mouth opened into a big O. Brianna leaned closer.

"They just *left* yesterday—both of them," Callie was saying. "Like, too boring for me, I'm out of here. And went to the beach! My sister saw them."

"Imagine if we did that?" Steve said. "We'd be gone. Kicked out."

"Their last musical?" Callie said. "Six million bucks. At a *high school*. They don't have to lift a finger. It's all about the money."

"I guess if *we* got that, we'd feel pretty *special*, too."

Another cackle.

Brianna was ready to storm inside. But Charles grabbed her with one arm and dragged her away, around the corner of the building until they were out of sight.

"Did you *hear* that?" Brianna said. "*Stupid-rich? Six million dollars? All about the money?* What kind of crap is that?"

"Honey, do not get your tits in an uproar," Charles said.

"I hate that expression!"

"Me, too." Charles began pacing. "Look, let's just quietly go across the street and settle down and talk this out over a Häagen-Dazs bar."

As they wound their way quickly around the building, they nearly rammed into Mr. Little, who was headed the other way.

"Actors on break—a moving hazard!" he said in a jolly voice. "You are just the two I wanted to see. I've been meaning to ask how you're enjoying the summer."

"Fine, just fine," Brianna said.

Mr. Little looked dubious. "Oh, dear, something knits the raveled brow of care . . ."

"Shakespeare?" Bri guessed.

"We're just having a little trouble finding a way to be useful," Charles said.

"Well, personally I can think of a million things," Mr. Little said, tapping his chin. "*Especially* for someone as talented and capable as the daughter of Evangeline Glaser." He cocked his head at Charles. "And . . . ?"

"The son of Bernard Scopetta," Charles said.

"Two important and dangerous missions come to mind," Mr. Little said. "The first happens to be my own part-time volunteer assistant. Catherine, who had the job for the last year, just left for a paid position at Lincoln Center."

"Really?" Bri was impressed.

"I'm afraid this won't be glamorous," Mr. Little went on. "It's mostly running errands, helping in the office, copying, fetching coffee—but it also involves greeting the stars when they arrive for each show, talking to suppliers, and learning all about what I do—theatrical production. I think you would be perfect, Brianna."

A job? Away from Steve and the Sandy Shores Death Eaters? "Sure," Brianna said. "I mean, thank you so much!"

"What's the other job?" Charles said.

"Volunteer coordinator to find and organize a group of ushers," Mr. Little said. "Everyone in our last crew has either retired or quit, so it will involve recruiting, training, scheduling, et cetera. Have you had this sort of leadership experience, Bernard?"

"Yes!" Charles blurted. "Yes, I'd *love* to! I have the perfect source. My mom works with retirees."

"Splendid!"

"And it's *Charles*—"

"Now, Brianna, dear," Mr. Little said, putting his hands together. "Would you mind calling the printer about the fund-raising brochures? Oh, and while you're at it, would you order lunch for the cast and crew? We like Darwin's—sandwiches and whatnot—ah, hello, Max!"

The Roman-warrior lighting intern was walking purposefully toward the theater. "Good morning, Mr. Little. It's Marc."

"Yes, Marc—what would you say Brianna should order for the crew's lunch? Does anyone have any food allergies, strong preferences?"

Marc shrugged. "I don't think so. Turkey clubs, I guess. Everyone loves turkey clubs. See you."

"Well, there you have it," Mr. Little said. "Problem solved. Follow me, let's get the phone number."

As Mr. Little walked toward his office, Brianna and Charles followed close behind. Charles was so excited, he looked like he would explode. "Oh dear. Oh my. Do you realize what this means?"

"You get to eat a decent lunch?" Brianna said.

"No, darlin'." Charles snapped his fingers with each word. "I have my new Charlettes!"

9

June 25, 09:13 P.M.

Let_there_be_light: *zzzup sistah kc!*

changchangchang: dashiell, WE MISS YOU SOO MUCH!

Let_there_be_light: *ditto. are things improving? getting to know the interns?*

changchangchang: well, it's only been two days. we found out three of them are vegans, though. brianna ordered turkey clubs for the crew.

Let_there_be_light: *ugh.*

changchangchang: the girls acted like she had personally strangled the turkeys.

changchangchang: they made a big show of taking out the meat, wiping off the rolls, and eating lettuce sandwiches.

Let_there_be_light: you could always come out to math camp. the people here eat anything. they don't talk to you though.

changchangchang: that would be an improvement, dash.

Let_there_be_light: oooooooh, i luv when you call me dash.

Let_there_be_light: i dont know if ive said this, but if anything ever happens between you and chip . . .

changchangchang: dashiell!!!!

Let_there_be_light: urps . . .

And breathe . . .

Reese lowered her forehead slowly down to her left calf, breathing in the smell of the freshly cut grass on the lawn between the theater and the dressing rooms.

As she rose back up she saw Shawn's door open. He had his own little room, unlike the rest of the cast in the "ensemble" dressing room. In a way, she felt bad for him. The cast dressing room was a hotbed of gossip and fun.

He began pacing back and forth, reading his script. She tried not to stare, letting her head fall until she could see the walkway behind her. Three male Sandy Shores interns were ogling her, their hair falling in front of their sweaty acne-covered faces.

She wiggled her butt, and they zoomed inside.

Shawn hadn't noticed the move.

Shawn hadn't noticed much about her over the last two days. Maybe he was embarrassed by the dance lesson on Tuesday. Since then he had acted as if he barely remembered her.

She yawned and realized her breath felt a little too cheese omeletty for her taste. Sitting upright in the stretch position, she leaned back to her shoulder bag and unzipped it, reaching in for a pack of mints. A smiling Shawn, on the cover of *People* magazine, peeked out— she hadn't been able to resist buying it at the Grand Union.

Quickly she turned the magazine over, burying it under the towel, makeup bag, sunscreen, sunglasses, candy bars, and iPod. Popping a mint into her mouth, she stuffed the tin back into the bag and stretched over her right leg.

And breathe . . .

"Three hundred ninety-seven . . . three hundred ninety-eight . . ." Charles sang, rushing by with Harrison. "We are not obvious, are we, Reesey dear?"

"*Charles!*"

" 'Eat your hearts out, I danced *with Shawn Nolan*,' " Harrison whispered breathlessly, reciting more or less what Reese had written on the Nolanfan.com blog the night before.

"I hate you both." Reese jumped to her feet, grabbed her shoulder bag, and raced after them. As they ran toward the theater door, laughing, she swung the bag.

The contents spilled out behind her, fanning out onto the grass.

"What happened?" asked a voice behind her.

Reese spun around. Shawn was walking in her direction, looking at the debris. On the grass next to her, his face was peeking up at her, among the junk from her bag. "Nothing," Reese said, quickly kicking her towel over the magazine.

"I'll get this," Shawn said, kneeling to pick up the makeup bag and sunscreen.

Reese scooped up the towel, with the magazine inside, and shoved them into the bag. "Thanks, Shawn. Sorry to interrupt your—whatever you were doing . . ."

Shawn sighed. "Memorizing. Also trying to do the accent. Around the caw-nuhr."

"The what?" Reese said.

"Corner. *Caw-nuhr.* I can't do the New York thing. I'm an L.A. guy."

"Well, you have to drop that last *r,*" Reese suggested.

"*Caw-nuh.*" Shawn made a hopeless face. "That still sucks."

"Maybe you don't *have* to do the accent," Reese said. "I have this cousin in Braintree—that's near Boston. They did a production of it there. Maria was Korean, Tony was Pakistani, and all the Jets and the Sharks sounded like Kennedys. Everybody loved it."

"PLACES FOR ACT ONE, SCENE FIVE!" Steve called from the theater door. "BRIDAL SHOP INTO 'AMERICA.'" Seeing Shawn, he gave a quick, sharp salute and said, "Let me know if you need my help, Mr. Nolan," then ducked back inside.

"Mr. Nolan?" Reese echoed.

Shawn laughed. "I thought he was talking to my dad."

Actors began spilling out of the dressing rooms for the start of the day's rehearsal, shouting and laughing. The guys were bony, tough-looking types, and one of them ran to Shawn and put his arm around his shoulder. He had frosty blue-green eyes that were almost wolflike. "Tony, my man, we're gonna rock it tonight!" he said, then did a theatrical double take at Reese. "Who's Babelicious?"

"Reese, this is Kenny, who's playing Riff, Tony's best bud," Shawn said—and as he did, a tall, black-haired girl with superlong legs reached seductively around Shawn's shoulders. "Oh, and this is Rosie, who plays Maria's best friend, Anita—"

"And can't resist my body," Kenny added.

Rosie rolled her eyes. "Watch out for him, Reese," she said. "He may be stupid, but he's ugly."

Shawn was waving over three more cast members, whom Reese recognized from the head shots she had seen in the program. "This is Marisol, who plays our lead, Maria," Shawn said. "And Lacey, who's a Shark girl but also Marisol's understudy—and José, our Bernardo, the leader of the Sharks who is also Maria's brother. Got that?"

"I think so," Reese said, shaking hands with all of them. Lacey was sweet and friendly with a round, open face. José had a handsome, sculpted face and a deep voice that seemed to rumble the ground; he bowed and kissed her hand when he shook it, folding his tall frame so his thick brown-black hair fell forward. Marisol had perfect golden skin, thick black hair pulled back in a ballet dancer's bun, and enormous brown eyes that radiated kindness.

"You live in the city?" Marisol asked.

"I'm a student," Reese said.

"NYU?" José asked.

"High school," Shawn said.

"No way!" Kenny said. "You're one of the *interns*?"

"Um, not exactly," Reese said, quickly adding, "but I'm eighteen."

No one laughed in disbelief. A couple of extra years wouldn't make a difference to strangers. Some lies were perfectly harmless.

"Are you guys coming to the party tomorrow night?" Rosie asked.

Party?

Reese looked at Shawn. "I haven't been invited—"

"It's for the whole cast, and you're part of the cast," Shawn said. "Bring your pals, too. It's at this beach house where I'm staying—belongs to the theater, right on the water. Can you guys come?"

ARE YOU KIDDING? OF COURSE! screamed Reese's mind. "I'll ask them," she said casually.

As they walked into the theater, Steve was standing inside the door. Reese gave him a great big smile.

What he didn't know wouldn't hurt him.

"A what?" Mr. Little asked, leaning over Brianna's shoulder and staring bewildered at the spreadsheet showing on the computer monitor.

"A scenario," Brianna said. "I set up these work sheets for your next fiscal year's budget, with different scenarios. So you can see projected profit and loss if you do the permanent waterproofing project. Or replace the tent. Or cut the orchestra by one musician—which I hope you don't—and any combination of the above over the next three years . . ."

She plugged numbers into her spreadsheet so Mr. Little could see how the results changed. "Amazing . . ." he said, glancing at his watch. "I have a meeting now. How about you take an hour break and come back afterward to give me a training session?"

"Sure," Brianna said.

As she walked out of the office and into the antechamber, she felt light on her feet. She liked impressing Mr. Little, although there had been a whole list of other things to do that she hadn't even touched. Like ordering lunches. Vegan lunches. Brianna had never seen so many vegans in her life. The discarded turkey slices from the sandwiches she'd ordered could have fed a small third-world village, and the burning glares that she had gotten from some of the other interns could have fried the bacon to a crisp. She would never accept culinary advice from Marc again.

Charles had parked himself at a small desk, talking on the theater's phone. "Goooood morning, Quail Hollow Assisted Living Facility! This is Mr. Scopetta of the Sandy Shores Playhouse, celebrating our half centennial! I know many of your residents and staff have been longtime theatergoers, and we have a wonderful opportunity for you or anyone you know—free plays all summer long if you join our spanking new usher crew!"

Giving him a little wave, Brianna stepped out into the still-cool late morning. She was dying to see the rehearsal. She started toward the tent, thinking about how when she was much younger, she used to sneak into the back row while her mom was having meetings and stare at the smiling faces and perfect bodies. She remembered wondering how human beings could possibly be so beautiful.

Ducking into the theater, she took a seat in the back.

The actors were finishing up the song "America"—the Puerto Rican immigrants singing joyously (and sarcastically) about living in America. She remembered the Playhouse's last production of *West Side Story*—how old was she then, eight? Nine? Different actors but just as magical now. Brianna started to applaud, and then her hands froze.

There they were, Harrison and Reese, right in the midst. Gorgeous, too—"shining it on," as her dad would say. As if their faces had been Photoshopped onto a memory.

It hurt. It really did hurt to be here when they were there.

Shove it out of your mind, she told herself.

"Okay, let's take a short break and come back with Act One, Scene Six!" Mr. Bishop called out.

Some of the Sharks climbed off the stage, while others lingered to review dance moves and song parts. Reese broke away and ran up the ramp. "Brianna!" she said in a hushed voice. "What are you doing tonight? Want to come to a party? Shawn's having a beach party for the cast—a cookout! I asked him if I could bring you and Charles and Casey, and he said yes—"

She broke off in midsentence, looking up toward the tent-flap exit.

Brianna turned. Steve was standing there, clutching

his clipboard, glaring. "I don't mean to interrupt," he said, "but it's almost lunchtime. Brianna, I'm not seeing the lunch delivery. It's usually here by now."

"Oh God!" Brianna leaped to her feet. She knew she was supposed to have done *something*. "Sorry, Steve, I got busy with another project—"

"Uh-huh," Steve said. "And don't forget—"

"Vegan dishes, right. I know. Last time they acted like I was trying to poison them."

Steve looked haggard and frustrated. "If this is too much for you, I can get someone else to do the job—"

Brianna shoved past him and headed up the aisle. "I can do it, Steve. I *forgot* to make the order, okay? Don't you forget sometimes?"

She stormed out of the theater, not waiting to hear Steve's muttered response.

10

"PARTYYYY!" SCREAMED KYLE, JOGGING AROUND the side of the house toward the gathering.

Casey squinted against the waning light and grinned. She had left a message about the party on Kyle's cell but wasn't sure he had gotten it. She waved to him and he waved back with his free hand. Under his other arm was a huge box whose label she could barely read . . . "Is that a box of beer?" she murmured.

"That would be a *case*," said Brianna, staking out a huge spot in the sand with a beach towel that said YALE 25ᵀᴴ REUNION—GO BULLDOGS! "And I hope not, considering this house is owned by my mom—so she's the one who gets in trouble if . . ."

"Oh dear," said Charles, carefully setting up a canvas

chair with drink holders in the armrests, under a giant umbrella in garish colors. "Entire cast of *West Side Story* jailed for promoting underage drinking, details at eleven!"

Harrison ran out toward Kyle. "Yo, what are you doing, trying to get us busted?"

"It's sodas, dude," Kyle replied with a laugh.

Casey looked around at the gorgeous vista and the modern shingled house with its wide glass windows, seeming to hover in the air on high, sturdy wood stilts. "You *own* this, but you don't spend the summers here anymore?"

"We lease it to the theater now," Brianna said with a shrug. "Mom and Dad have a nicer place in Sag. I'm starving. Are there any burgers ready?"

Sag.

That must be Sag Harbor. Casey, who had moved to Ridgeport last fall, was still trying to get used to the Long Island lingo. She smoothed out her own blanket, taking care to pin the corners down with shoes, a shoulder bag, and her own cooler. Brianna had joined Shawn, Marisol, and a couple of other actors gathered by a giant barbecue pit that was lined with rocks. A few others were setting up a boom box on a blanket, while still another group unpacked meat, corn, veggies, and drinks from a huge cooler. In the distance Casey could hear a few laughing voices far out in the surf.

Dropping the case of sodas in the sand, Kyle ran toward Shawn. "*Duuuuuude!*" he cried out. "*You were the bomb in* Battle Lines!"

Shawn spun around, immediately backing away. "Uh, thanks—but I think that was Shawn *Moore*."

"Oh. Really?" Kyle stopped short. "Damn, I get you guys mixed up."

Rosie, who had been ostentatiously following Kyle with her eyes, edged closer, with a sexy smile. "Do people mix *you* up with anyone?"

"He has a hard enough time remembering his own name," Charles remarked.

Kyle immediately grabbed a handful of ice and put it down the back of Charles's shirt, sending him off shrieking.

Casey smiled. Everyone loved Kyle.

As she settled down on the towel, unpacking a couple of magazines to read while there was still light, Kyle plopped himself down on the smoothed fabric. "'Sup, Case? Great party. Thanks for calling me."

"Shawn said to invite all our friends," Casey said with a shrug.

Kyle took off his shirt and lay back, breathing deeply. "I did seven and a half miles today. Plus two hundred crunches. Can you tell?"

He was angling himself toward her and stiffening—*flexing*, whatever you called it—his abs. They looked like they had lives of their own, trapped tubular creatures beneath the skin.

She looked away. What was she supposed to say to that? *Why was he doing this?* "Um . . . yes. I mean, I guess. I mean, um, good work . . ."

Good work?

She had a vocabulary. A good one. But whenever he was around, the words just dried up and flew away. Talking to his face was hard enough. But talking to his face-and-naked-torso was just *not fair*.

He thinks I'm an idiot, she thought.

She should have been comfortable. She and Kyle had shared . . . well, *something*. That miserable brooding night by the duck pond, early in the year when Casey had been so scared and lonely, he'd actually kissed her—just appeared out of the blue to lift her out of one of the darkest hours of her life. Which may have tied her to him forever, had she not found him hooking up with Reese that same night. Which should have been cause for violence. But Kyle was Kyle. You could hate him for about a day or a week. Somehow he always won you back. Like the puppy who tears up your favorite book and then comes back with bewildered, sorrowful eyes.

You not only give in, you want to go straight for the treats.

"I think I can double it by football season," he said, panting in loud bursts as he quickly convulsed his body into a few more crunches.

"Will you stop that?" Charles said, still shaking the ice from his shirt. "I'm exhausted watching."

A couple of the actors broke into wild applause as he finished, and Kyle hopped up to take a bow. Just beyond the pit, Casey saw Brianna and Harrison chatting intently.

Kyle grabbed a couple of bottled waters from a cooler, offering one as he sat back down next to Casey. "How's the Chipmeister?" he asked.

Casey sighed. "Too far away."

"Bummer," he said.

As the smell of cooking hamburgers wafted around them and the original cast album of West Side Story blared from the boom-box speakers, they watched the sun slowly sink, leaving an amber trail as if spilling out its contents into the sea.

"Now, *that* looks cool," Kyle said, leaning back so his shoulder rested against hers.

Casey tensed. He had just mentioned Chip—what was this all about?

But Kyle was staring out to the horizon with a rapturous grin. She knew what it was about. It was about the horizon. And the fact that Kyle was a serial, equal-opportunity nuzzler. It didn't mean a thing. Besides, pulling away would have been hostile and dumb. And his big old body just felt so . . . comfy.

She let her head drop until it rested on his shoulder. He shifted so that the little hollow there became like a welcoming soft pillow.

"Wow," he said, looking out to sea.

Casey smiled into the summer night.

Her feeling exactly.

11

"*MARIAAAAAAAA!*" HARRISON SCREAMED ON AN
impossibly high pitch in an impossibly ugly, loud voice.

"Kill it!" shouted one of the actors.

Reese had never seen Harrison like this. The party had
ended, and now everyone was headed in the direction
of the house. Some were laughing and singing, others
huddled arm in arm in soft intimate conversation—or
gathered around Shawn, who was doing what he'd been
doing all night, answering questions about Hollywood.
Harrison, it seemed, was in his own world.

"What got into Greek boy?" Charles asked.

"Beer," said Brianna. "I guess no one carded him."

Reese grinned. "He's cute when he's drunk . . ."

"Dude, he only had *one*," Kyle said with a laugh.

"I'm not a dude," Reese replied, "and I can prove it."

Kyle backed off. "Whoa, this is a PG party—"

Harrison sidled over to them with a self-satisfied smile. "That was my intim— imitation of Jerry Lewis doing Tony, doing 'Maria' . . ."

"Perfect!" Marisol said. "Get this man a karaoke mike."

"Yo, I know this great bar up the street . . ." José said.

The party was breaking up, and Reese had barely seen Shawn. Earlier, she had stood close to him for about two seconds, but he had been listening to something Marisol was saying, and hadn't really noticed her. Now she saw him talking to Kenny, the guy who was playing Riff. They were standing a few feet away from coolers that held all the drinks.

Slowly and deliberately, Reese walked closer, eyeing the coolers and trying to appear as if thirst was the first thing on her mind. She considered "accidentally" bumping up against Shawn, but that trick was old—"I do my own stunts" was the kind of line you couldn't use twice. She bent over, rummaging through the few remaining soda cans, aware that she was wearing extremely short cutoffs and wondering if Shawn noticed.

She retrieved a diet soda then stood up and felt someone come up behind her.

"Hey." It was Shawn's voice, low and sexy and raw in the night air.

He'd noticed.

"Hey," she responded, telling herself to play it cool.

"Enjoying the party?" he asked.

She turned to face him. "Yeah. How about you?"

"It's been okay. But it's better now." Even under the night sky, that smile seemed to reach straight into her heart. "Have you been here the whole time?"

"For a couple of hours."

"And I've spent nearly the whole party talking to José and Rosie and Marisol," he said, shaking his head. "How'd that happen?"

Reese didn't answer. She was pretty sure the question was rhetorical.

Shawn scratched his head. "How about if you give me a rain check?"

"A rain check?"

"Yeah. A promise that in the very near future, I can spend some time talking to you."

Reese couldn't answer at first. Her breath seemed stuck in the pit of her stomach. "I think," she finally said, "I can manage that."

"I'll hold you to it," he promised, then bounced away, turning to face the rest of the party. "Dudes, I'm heading to bed! I have to get to the theater early tomorrow . . ."

"Tomorrow's Saturday, right?" José said. "Didn't they call a two o'clock rehearsal on Saturday?"

Shawn shrugged. "I'm a workaholic, dude. See you guys."

After a chorus of groans and reluctant good-byes, the others headed around the house to the front, where the cars were parked.

Reese stood there, as if the sand had turned to cement. What had just happened?

A *rain check?* He wanted a rain check—for *her!*

She swallowed hard. It was something. She didn't know what it meant, but it was something. And she suddenly felt a big, ridiculous grin growing across her face, which, if it hadn't been dark out, would probably have drawn everyone's concern for her sanity.

Reese watched Shawn walk toward the beach house. He had a rocking, slightly bowlegged gait. She hadn't realized how sexy that was. She wondered what the house was like inside. She wondered what he would have said if she had joined him. She wondered what would happen when he cashed in on his rain check.

Uh-uh-uh, put it out of your mind, she told herself. *He said he wanted to talk. Just talk. Keep a lid.*

He'd been flirting, that's all. It didn't necessarily mean anything. Time to go. To think about important things. Like working on her tan tomorrow. "Who wants to go to the beach in the morning?" she asked.

"Me," Brianna said.

"I'm there," Charles replied.

"Hey." Harrison stopped at the edge of the group of cars. "Where's my car? *Someone stole my car!*"

"Uh, Harrison, you did not drive, *I* did," Brianna said, "and you are *very* lucky I am agreeing to drive you back, so if you have even the slightest idea of getting sick . . ." Brianna stopped just short of her silver Honda. "What the—?"

On the passenger seat was a crumpled-up McDonald's bag and a half-eaten salad. A spilled bag of croutons littered the carpet. "Harrison, did you eat a McDonald's meal on the way down here?"

"No . . ." Harrison said, staring at the debris.

Brianna swept everything onto the pavement. "Next time I will not leave the windows open."

"I have some trash bags in my car," Reese volunteered. But as she walked over to her blue convertible VW, her heart began racing. The top was down, and something was on the seats. "Uh, guys . . . ?"

Casey was the first to run over. She leaned in to the car and reached in. "It's sand . . . someone poured sand all over the seats."

"Vanilla!" came a disgusted shout from Charles to their left. He was standing by his parents' minivan, holding his right hand up, his fingers spread. "There's vanilla milk shake all over my door handles."

"José, Kenny . . . Marisol?" Reese called out to the other actors parked nearby. "Did somebody mess up your cars?"

"No," came the three responses.

"It's only us," Charles said. "Someone did this to us."

"*It was Chiiiiino!*" Harrison said in his earsplitting voice. "Let's have a *rrru-u-u-mmble!*"

"Easy, Jerry," Charles said, "this is serious."

Reese handed Harrison some plastic bags. "Use your hands for something constructive for a change."

"The interns," Brianna said. "That's who did it."

"Were they here?" Reese asked.

"I didn't see them," Charles said.

"We're pretty close to the street," Casey said. "It could have been some random jerks—"

"Not in this neighborhood," Brianna said. "The interns

know where this address is—it's the official 'star's residence' for each play. They knew about the party, too."

"But that's—" Casey began.

"Babyish?" Brianna said. "Hey, we were invited and they weren't."

"They haven't exactly been happy campers before this," Charles pointed out.

"Yo, my car's okay!" Kyle announced brightly.

"You're not in the show," Brianna shot back, digging a flashlight out of her glove compartment to scan for more garbage. "I'm going to confront them tomorrow at the theater. And if I find out they did it, I will make them lick my carpet clean."

Charles was carefully rubbing his door handles with a wet wipe. "Darlin', I'd buy tickets to see that. . . ."

In her air-conditioned bedroom, the residual drops of water from her shower felt tickly cool on Reese's shoulder. She tied her hair back with a scrunchy and sat at her desk. Her fingers flew over the keyboard, pulling up her current home page:

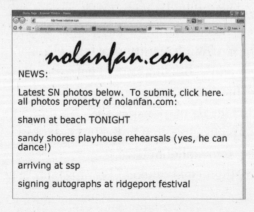

nolanfan.com

NEWS:

Latest SN photos below. To submit, click here.
all photos property of nolanfan.com:

shawn at beach TONIGHT

sandy shores playhouse rehearsals (yes, he can dance!)

arriving at ssp

signing autographs at ridgeport festival

She focused on the top line.

"Oh . . . my . . . God . . ." she murmured.

Quickly she tapped out Charles's number on her cell.

He answered on the fifth ring with a groggy voice. "You've got to be joking . . ."

"Are you asleep? I didn't mean to—"

"You don't mean to. Brianna doesn't mean to. Casey doesn't mean to. But you all do it anyway. It's the latest sport, calling Charles just when he's settled into a sensational dream. Damn it, Reese, I was choreographing a kick line with my geriatric ushers."

"Sounds hot."

"It wasn't. And if this conversation isn't either, doll, there will be hell to pay."

"They posted photos. On nolanfan."

"*Of my ushers?*"

"Of the beach party, Charles! You're in them, and so am I."

"How do I look?"

"Don't you get it? Think back. Who had a camera at the party?"

"*Everybody*. Who doesn't have a cell phone?"

"But, Charles, all the photos had the sea in the background, which means they were taken from the house. So who took the pictures? Where were they?"

"Maybe Shawn has a trusty houseboy—"

"It's a *spy*, Charles. Whoever trashed our cars took these photos."

"Hmm. You think—"

"The interns. We have to figure out which one of them visits nolanfan. It says, 'Photos posted by cuspbaby08.'"

"The cusp . . . aha! That's it, Reese. We find someone who was born on the cusp of the eighth month . . . August—"

"And then we have our culprit."

"And we plot our revenge . . . ooh, I can involve my Charlushers in this, too!"

"*Charlushers?*"

"Maybe I need to work on the name?"

"Good night, Charles."

"Good night, Sherlock. I love you."

Click.

Reese zoomed in on the beach photo, at the scene by the barbecue pit. Shawn was next to her, in profile. Laughing. He'd actually been laughing at Marisol's joke, but it seemed as if he was looking at Reese. And touching her arm.

She right-clicked and saved the photo to her hard drive.

Shawn . . . Shawn . . . Shawn . . . Shawn . . .

Shawn and Reese at the beach.

She fell asleep with a smile.

12

BEACH, BEACH, BEACH.

Reese breathed in the warm, salty air and felt the sun roast her cheeks as she crossed the sand. This was one of the best parts of living on Long Island—summer weekends, where you could party at the beach at night and then follow up the next morning with . . . a trip to the beach.

Next to her, Charles stopped short. His arms, loaded with a cooler, an umbrella, several beach blankets, and a bag full of magazines, seemed to sag. "I don't believe it. They're here."

Reese squinted into the morning sun at the swarm of bodies near the lifeguard stand, just in front of them. The Sandy Shores interns, nearly *all* of them, were staking out one of the only remaining uninhabited patches of sand.

"This is not a bad thing, Charles," she said. "We can do some research."

"Ah, yes . . . Cuspbaby," Charles said in a conspiratorial whisper. "The game is afoot."

Brianna, who had arrived in her car just behind them, strolled up beside them, along with Casey and a very groggy-looking Harrison. Brianna adjusted her Dolce & Gabbana sunglasses, staring at the interns. "Oh, gulp. Do we sit near them to appear friendly or go far away to have a much better time?"

"Let's compromise and stay right here," Charles said. "You all go swim. I'll stay, cultivate my tan, and make sure our blanket does not collect their garbage."

"Charles . . . the *research* . . ." Reese reminded him, marching toward the interns.

As the others followed her, a couple of the Sandy Shores kids looked up and said hello. Steve ignored them. He was teaching Callie how to dance the mambo.

"He's not bad," Reese mumbled, "for a techie."

"Guess he's another closeted frustrated Sandy Shores performer," Brianna said, dropping her Metropolitan Museum tote bag squarely on Harrison's right foot.

"I think that hurt . . ." Harrison rasped. "Which must mean I'm alive."

He sleepily unfurled his blanket, which hadn't been shaken out since the last time he used it—sending a spray of sand toward Callie, Lauren, and Amber. Callie screamed, covering her eyes.

"Dang, sorry," Harrison said. Callie and Lauren

worked in the costume shop, he reminded himself, but he couldn't remember where Amber was assigned.

"*Ow ow ow ow, I wear hard contacts,*" Callie cried out, her face twisted in pain.

"I'll help you take them out," Lauren said, gently sitting her down on a blanket.

"He didn't mean it," Reese said.

"Can't you guys go somewhere else?" Steve demanded.

"Funny, I was going to ask you the same thing," Brianna said.

"She didn't mean it," Reese said.

Immediately Charles piped up, "Anybody want to hear horoscopes?" He spread out a Miss Piggy towel and then pulled a newspaper from his shoulder bag. "I can*not* begin my day without the horoscopes."

Marc's eyes were fixed on the towel in an expression of horror. "Can you, like, turn that over or something?"

"Miss Piggy is my life role model," Charles said, unfurling his newspaper. "Let's start with you, Marc. What's your sign?"

"Sounds like a pickup line," Marc said with a snicker.

"Don't flatter yourself," Charles shot back. "Sorry. Joke. I *am* serious. Mmm, I'd say you were a Leo maybe. August. Like . . . on the cusp?"

Subtlety, Reese decided, was not Charles's strong suit.

"I'm a Taurus," Harrison said, grimacing as he lay on his beach blanket. "But today I feel like an old VW . . ."

"Hung over?" Callie asked.

"Can't imagine where they got the beer," said her friend Amber.

Aha! Reese leaned in closer. "How did you know it was beer?"

Amber and Callie gave her a look. "Huh?" Callie asked.

"How did you know," Reese said carefully, "that Harrison drank beer and not something else, like wine or, like, whiskey? How would you know that *unless you were there?*"

"He drinks *whiskey?*" Amber asked, her face curdling into disgust.

"No!" Reese said. "My question was about where you were last night."

"God, you sound like my mom," Callie said.

Charles nudged Reese. "Well, look at this. *Mine*—Libra—says, 'If you are honest to everyone, they will be honest to you.'"

"I'll start," Marc groaned. "I wish you'd be quiet. That's honest."

"Fine," Charles said, folding up his newspaper. "No problem. Just trying to be friendly."

"Oh God, give it a rest, Dorothy," Marc said.

"What did you call him?" Harrison said, looking up and shielding his eyes with his hand.

"Chill, it's an expression," Marc said.

"He calls everyone that," Callie added.

"How come I've never heard it?" Brianna asked.

"Maybe because you don't listen," Marc said with a laugh.

Now Harrison was rising from the sand. "Yo, you guys are out of line. Totally."

"Are you for real, dude?" Marc stood up, too, smiling defiantly.

The interns were on their feet now, too, circling around. Reese couldn't believe this. Not this early. She and Brianna stood up, scrambling to place themselves in front of Harrison and Charles.

But Steve beat them to it, stepping between Harrison and Marc. "Chill, both of you."

"They take over the acting roles, they work in the office," Marc said, gesturing angrily, "and now they're going to have the ushers doing a kick line down the aisle, dressed in feather boas."

Harrison charged past Steve, who grabbed him by the forearm and yanked him back with surprising force. "Easy, bud," he said, then turned back to Marc. "I think you should apologize."

"What?" Marc said in utter shock.

Steve was staring intently at Marc. "Just because they're treating us like crap, it doesn't mean we stoop to their level. Now apologize."

"But—"

"I'm in charge of the interns. And if I tell Mr. Little you're out, that's it. Your ass is grass."

Reese and Brianna exchanged looks of astonishment. Marc stared at Steve, speechless, his face twisted with confusion and anger.

Finally he murmured, "Sorry."

"He has a name," Steve said.

For a moment Marc's eyes flashed—but if he'd had any sudden smart comment, he swallowed it. "Sorry, Charles," he said.

"No worries," Charles replied. "And FYI, I am not using feather boas. At least, not for this show."

Brianna saw a familiar figure approach through the office window. Quickly she saved the customer database on Mr. Little's computer and ran outside.

Steve was rushing toward the theater, flipping pages in a clipboard as he went. She took a deep breath and called out, "Steve?"

He turned. "Yeah?"

"I—I just wanted to thank you," she said, managing a smile. "That was a nice thing you did this morning. Sticking up for Charles."

Steve's features softened slightly. He looked down. "Oh. No problem."

"Not that he needs it. I mean, he can stick up for himself, big-time. But in a big crowd like that . . ."

"Cool," Steve said, turning away.

"Wait," Brianna called out. "Can I ask you one thing?"

"I'm supposed to be inside in two minutes."

"Um, what did you mean when you said we were treating you like crap?"

Steve spun to face her. "What—?"

"That's what you said. To Marc. Just because we were treating you like crap . . ."

Steve glanced at his watch and thought a moment.

"Okay. Every year we have this preseason meeting where interns talk about what they want. So this year, turns out everyone wants to do sets—*everyone*. But I have to assign people to props and costumes, and three guys quit. So I make some phone calls, find three more, and get all the jobs assigned. Somehow I take care of all the tantrums and hurt feelings. Everything is going well. The summer is planned out. And then, out of the blue, you guys show up—and not only do they let your friends be *in* the show, but it looks like you all expect everything to be handed to you. Like you can pick and choose flavors of ice cream— 'Do I want to act or build or paint?' Like we're nothing."

"We didn't mean to be that way."

"You guys are famous," Steve said. "We all know that. Everyone in our school read the article in the *Times*. We don't have the reputation, or the budget. But we live here in Sandy Shores, and this is *our* theater. Every year we look forward to the summer. It's *our* time. Look, I just want to be fair, Brianna, that's all. And help put on a great season."

His small brown eyes seemed to have grown. They were deep and liquid, his bony face calmer than she had ever seen it. With a quick, almost nervous gesture, he tucked a lock of his long blond hair behind his ears, and in the afternoon sun it seemed to have streaks of red.

"We're not as bad as you think," Brianna said. "It's hard to walk into a closed shop. Snobbery works both ways, you know."

Steve shrugged. "Yeah. You're right about that, I guess."

"Can I ask a question and get an honest answer?"

"I do honest answers all the time. I get in trouble for it."

"That makes two of us." Brianna smiled. "Last night, at Shawn's house? Some of our cars were trashed. Do you know anything about it?"

"No," Steve said, shaking his head. "I was playing ball with Marc and a couple of other interns. No. We did not do it, if that's what you're wondering."

"Okay," Brianna said. "Just curious."

Steve smiled, and his face softened. For the first time, Brianna could see a trace of hurt in his expression—hurt that anyone would suspect him of trashing a car. He was telling the truth, somehow she knew it. He was all about honor. Maybe too much.

Which reminded her of someone she knew. Like herself.

"Well," he said as if to back away

But he didn't. And Brianna hadn't expected him to. And those two facts seemed to have a physics of their own, a special Law of Attraction regarding two bodies at rest and gravitational pull—

And there he was looming closer, and like any force of nature, all you could do was give in. You weren't thinking *this does not compute* and backing off. Or *oh, this is a kiss* and trying to do it the best way. It just happened—his arms around her, his lips—and the shock of it, the feeling of no control, made Brianna pull away.

And her thoughts, scattered about like buckshot, now began to coalesce into something like logic, something that was looming over her, scolding. *What on earth do you think you're doing?*

"Um . . ." she said, looking around to see if they'd been spotted. Luckily, they were shielded from view by the side of Mr. Little's office.

She looked at him as if doing so would instantly rewind the whole thing. It couldn't have happened.

Steve?

He smiled. And then he began to laugh.

Brianna's eyes darted away, as if he'd seen her naked. Part of her wanted to feel betrayed and angry. But that part felt hollow now. He wasn't laughing at her. He was laughing at the insanity of what had just happened.

She felt her lips turning up, a snortish, laughish sound hissing from them.

"That was—" he said.

"A mistake," Brianna replied.

Steve exhaled and shrugged. "Sorry."

"No problem."

He began whistling "Somewhere," and disappeared into the theater.

Mr. Little poked his head out from inside the office. "Maybe 'Hello, Young Lovers' would be more appropriate?"

Brianna burst out laughing. "Yeah. In a million years."

It was theater. In the theater, you did crazy things. It didn't mean anything.

He was a jerk. She had slipped. No big deal.

She headed back to her desk. Time to work. Lots to do.

But as she jiggled her mouse and the screen came to

life, she wasn't really focusing on the screen. She could, however, see her own reflection.

Faintly.

Well, except for the smile.

13

"HE WHAT?" REESE ASKED, STRETCHING OUT ON the floor next to Brianna's desk.

"Apologized," Brianna said. "Sort of."

"*Steve*? Are you sure it wasn't his kindly twin?"

"No! I mean, yes! It happened just like three minutes ago. Reese, I am full of revelations this morning. Number one, Steve is all about the work. That's it. I don't think he's a complete jerk."

"Okay, maybe eighty-five percent?" Reese said.

"Number two—"

The front door burst open and Marisol rushed through the outer office. "Oh my God oh my God oh my God oh my God oh my God . . ." she murmured, ignoring Brianna, stepping over Reese, and disappearing into Mr.

Little's office without shutting the door behind her.

Reese gave Brianna a glance, but she just shrugged.

Together they sneaked closer to the open door. They strained to listen, but with the buzz of the air conditioners, they could only hear breathless snatches of Marisol's voice: "Audition in L.A. . . . pilot . . . leading role . . . she wins a singing contest and gets recruited into a sting operation . . . comedy . . . mystery . . . incredible opportunity . . ."

In a moment Mr. Little's office fell silent. When he finally spoke, his voice was boomy and clear. "Well, Marianne, we do have only two weeks of rehearsal, and there is no out in the contract for extended absence . . ."

"Marisol . . ." she corrected him. "I know I know I know I know . . . feel like such a jerk . . . once in a lifetime . . . only an audition . . . be back in time for the first performance . . ."

Suddenly the door closed. Brianna and Reese snapped back to where they were. "Oh my God," Reese whispered. "What if she gets the part?"

"She'll come back and do Maria, then after the show closes she'll go back to L.A. to shoot the TV show," Brianna said with a shrug. "People don't get cast in TV shows and then have to start work *the next day* . . . do they?"

"What if they do?"

Brianna shrugged again. "Her understudy would take over—Lacey."

And Lacey's spot in the ensemble would open up, Reese thought.

And that spot would need to be filled.

And the swing would fill it.

"I know what you're thinking . . ." Brianna said with a smile.

The door to Mr. Little's office opened a bit, and he peered out. "Brianna? Can you call in Lucy for a moment? And, Reese, I'm glad you're here. Please stay, you'll be involved in this, too. Marisol will be missing a few rehearsals, and we will need to make some temporary adjustments."

Marisol, her eyes teary, appeared behind him, looking both scared and thrilled.

"I'll get, um, *Lacey* right away," Brianna said. She squeezed Reese's hand, jumping up from her seat and running out the door.

"Well, dear," Mr. Little said to Reese with a big smile. "It looks like you will be taking over a role for the remainder of the rehearsal period."

Reese nodded soberly.

In her mind, she was shrieking.

"You're going to be *Lacey*?" Charles asked, hands on each side of his face.

Reese tried to be calm. She nodded. "The character is Teresita. She sings solos in 'America' *and* 'I Feel Pretty'— and she has lines—*and* a featured dance bit!"

Charles looked at her. She looked at him.

"AGGHHHHH!"

She couldn't see. She couldn't feel her feet touching the ground. This was IT—she had made it. Okay, it was only for rehearsals, but it was a role, a real role, *in a professional theater*!

"AGGHHHHH!"

Charles was screaming, too, almost as loud as Reese. His face was red. They were jumping together, his arms around her, right in front of the theater exit. Who cared if people saw them?

"Okay. Okay," Reese said, catching her breath. "It's only until Marisol comes back. It's not really a big deal."

"Unless she gets the TV role," Charles said. "Or dies in a tragic plane crash."

"Charles!"

"We have to prepare for everything. Are they making you a costume? Lacey is bigger than you."

"I don't need a costume. Marisol is *returning*!"

"Not till opening night, dear." Charles took Reese by the arm and started walking toward the costume shop. "Which means you may be doing dress rehearsal. And I will *not* have Teresita Van Cleve, International Star, appearing onstage in a shapeless sack."

He knocked on the door and entered. The costume shop was cramped and smelled of mildew and wet plaster. An enormous exhaust fan whirred in the window, and Lauren sat at a small table piled high with festive skirts and spangled vests. "I know, I know, we heard," said Lauren, without looking up. "What's your size?"

"Four," said Reese.

"Well, *that* sucks." Lauren scowled. "Can you eat a lot of junk food this week?"

"You could make the dresses adjustable," Charles

suggested. "To prepare for the event that Marisol does *not* return."

"If we hear that she isn't, we'll adjust then, no prob," Lauren said. "That's what we're here for."

"You will? At the last minute? You'll let out *all* of Marisol's costumes, and take in *all* of Lacey's?" Charles said. "And think about dress rehearsal—Lacey will rip her seams and Reese will look like a poor refugee from Anatevka!"

"Uh, what would you suggest we do?" Lauren asked, looking at Charles as if he had three heads.

"Look," he said, picking up one of the costumes and turning it around. "What if some of these party dresses have lace in the back—very appropriate for the fifties, very Eisenhowerish-New-Victorian-whatever. For Lacey's and Marisol's duds we put an insert from neck to tush. Pull on the lace . . . let it out . . . everyone looks miraculously perfect!"

Reese grinned. It was a great idea. And simple.

Charles handed Lauren the costume and she placed it back on the pile. "Thanks, that's an interesting concept," she said.

"Where's Ms. Gruber?" Charles asked. "Er, Ariel. I'll tell her—"

"I hear the ushers are arriving today," Lauren interrupted.

"Uh . . . yeah, at two o'clock," Charles replied. "For a meeting."

Lauren gave him a withering look. "You take care of the ushers. And we'll take care of the costumes."

"But—" Charles said.

Reese pulled Charles by the sleeve toward the door. "Thanks, Lauren."

"No prob," Lauren replied. "Good luck."

"What are you *doing*?" Charles said, stumbling outside. "She has no right to do this. She's an intern. I'm going straight to Ariel Gruber—"

"No," Reese said. "Don't do it, Charles. Let them learn from their own mistakes. This is not about being right, Charles. It's about getting along."

Charles put his hands on his hips. "And since when have we been living Muppet values?"

Reese gave him a kiss on the cheek. "I love you."

"Places for Act Two, Scene One, 'I Feel Pretty'!" Steve shouted from the tent opening.

"That's me!" Reese's insides clenched. "Come watch?"

"I'll cry," Charles said.

They scurried inside. The dancers were gathering onstage. Mr. Fredericks was playing softly on the piano while Steve stood by scribbling on his clipboard.

Brianna was next to him, pointing something out. Together they broke into laughter.

"Do you see what I see?" Charles murmured out of the side of his mouth.

Reese took both sides of his face and turned his head toward the stage. "Will you ignore them? Pay attention, please. A star is born."

14

June 28, 10:11 P.M.

SCOPASCETIC: *have u given up?*

dancerslut: i screwed up america.

SCOPASCETIC: *i don't mean THAT.*

dancerslut: u agree? i did screw it up?????

SCOPASCETIC: *u were FAB. i LOVED watching u. u know that.*

SCOPASCETIC: *ur changing the subject, doll. i meant about the photos. the jpegs from the beach? the trashing of the cars?*

dancerslut: i dunno. so much has happened . . .

SCOPASCETIC: *give me back your nancy drew magnifying glass . . .*

dancerslut: hey, i heard u & the ushers cackling in the lobby. what r they doing, reading the aarp comics aloud?

SCOPASCETIC: i am not amused by that slur. we were rehearsing.

dancerslut: rehearsing????? what do ushers rehearse?

SCOPASCETIC: not ushers, CHARLUSHERS. i gave them choreography. they give out programs with this little florish (sp?) and then do a spin to the left before going to the seats. they crack me up.

dancerslut: they're like 80 yrs old.

SCOPASCETIC: one of them says shes 37. but she may be lying.

SCOPASCETIC: she is lying.

SCOPASCETIC: anyway i guess we were laughing too hard cuz that squeezably lovable steve caught us & told mr. little. so we're back to the boring stuff. and i cant bitch to anyone because ur too busy slobbering over shawn, and la glaser has gone over to the dark side.

dancerslut: ???????

SCOPASCETIC: she and steve.

dancerslut: ur dreaming.

SCOPASCETIC: well, it's a theory. u told me she said he wasn't so bad. & during rehearsal they were laughing etc. joined at the hip.

dancerslut: u have a wild imagination. she still hates him. she has taste. end of subject.

dancerslut: & if ur worried u can't bitch to anyone, u can always lean on me, honey.

SCOPASCETIC: *i luv u too.*

"And-a one, two, THREE!"

Mr. Fredericks tore into the dance break music for "America," and Reese began counting. It was all about numbers at this point. And turns. *Sharp. Sharp. Sharp.* And kicks. Reese had been distracted by Rosie, who was playing Anita and dancing hard, trying to keep up with the beat.

"YEOW!" shouted José suddenly, staggering across the set.

"Sorryyyy!" shouted Rosie, her eyes wide and her hand over her mouth.

"This is the only set of cojones I have!" José cried out in a high-pitched voice.

As the other dancers started laughing, Mr. Fredericks banged helplessly on the piano. "Break!" he shouted.

José limped offstage, contorted in mock agony. Rosie, with a hopeless sigh, shrugged at Mr. Bunt. "I can't get that rhythm!"

"You will," Mr. Bunt said amiably, fishing his cell phone out of his pocket. "You just have to feel it, babe. I'll be back in a minute."

"It's very Spanish," Mr. Fredericks said, backing up the ramp toward the door. "Two groups of six, the first in six-eight, the second in three quick twos."

"Uh-huh." Rosie turned toward Reese, throwing up her hands. "The one guy tells me to feel it, the other gives me

Music Theory 101. I'm a nice Irish-Italian singer from Manhasset. I can't do this."

Reese felt for Rosie. She was an amazing soprano. When she sang "A Boy Like That," she made the hairs rise on the back of Reese's neck. Rosie wasn't a bad dancer either, she just needed confidence. "It's hard to count it," Reese said. "I just think of it like this: *slow . . . slow . . . fast fast fast.*"

She did a couple of measures of the dance, and Rosie followed.

"Yes!" Reese said. "That's it!"

Rosie smiled. "Really? That's all?"

"Lookin' good!" came Shawn's voice from the back of the theater. "Hey, anyone available to run lines?"

Rosie's eyebrows were slowly creeping upward. "You go, *querida*," she said with a knowing look. "I need to practice. And thanks."

"Thanks . . ." Reese smiled, bounding off the stage.

As she ran toward the door, following Shawn, she could hear Rosie chanting "Slow . . . slow . . . fast fast fast."

Reese looked up at Shawn. "I believe you have a rain check," she reminded him.

"Oh . . . ?" Shawn tapped his chin. "Does running lines count—in my dressing room?"

"I'll have to think about that . . ." Reese replied, choking back the *ARE YOU KIDDING? YES!* that was at the tip of her tongue.

Shawn laughed. "It's got a/c," he said, walking out of the theater and across the walkway. "I'm burning up."

He pushed open his door, which had a cheap-looking

gold star tacked to it. A gust of cool air blasted outward. The cinderblock walls were lit by beautiful Art Deco sconces of translucent glass and covered with framed posters and photos from Sandy Shores Playhouse productions, signed by the stars. Shawn's mirror had photos tucked into the frame—Shawn with family, Shawn goofing with friends, Shawn arm in arm with different stars . . .

"Is that Christina Aguilera?" Reese asked.

Shawn laughed. "She's mad crazy, I love her. We did not go out, though, I don't care what the *Enquirer* said. She is so too old for me."

Reese could not help staring at all the familiar faces. He knew *everyone*.

"Sorry for the mess. Sit." He shoved a pile of clothes off a director's chair for Reese, and then plopped his script on the makeup table, sweeping aside an iPod, a paperback, a makeup kit, and a tube of zit cream. "Act One, Scene Seven always kills me," he said. "The bridal shop scene, where Tony and Maria are alone and sing about their love among the mannequins. Gag me. Did I say that? I didn't say that. Can you read Maria?"

Zit cream. Reese loved the fact that he needed the stuff. You couldn't tell. Not for a second.

Shawn cocked his head as he handed Reese the script. "What are you looking at?"

"Nothing!" Reese snapped to. "I just—I'm sorry. Act Seven . . . ?"

"Act One, Scene Seven."

His fingers brushed against hers as she took the script. In the plain choreography of life, the way things were *supposed* to work, he would have leaned back thoughtfully, waiting for Reese to feed him his cues. But he stayed leaning forward, stayed smiling, and Reese recognized the body language, she picked up the shift in the air—but this wasn't *really* real life, this was Shawn Nolan, Shawn who knew Christina and Pink and Justin and Gwen, Shawn whose smile and skin and body came from a different world with different rules. So she looked down, flipping through the pages as he leaned nearer, and it clicked in Reese's brain that he had brought her here for a reason and that she knew everything she needed to know, and how many sets of rules were there, anyway? Before she could analyze any further, she was feeling his lips, his arms, a silvery warmth that blasted open every pore in her body. Everything—the posters, the photos, the mirror, the walls—vanished into fog, and all that was left was a sense that every molecule of hers was wrapping itself around his, that there was only one world, one set of rules, and they were making them up as they went along.

Their lips didn't part so much as Reese felt a gentle stream of air slip between them, and she sighed a sound so feathery and fleeting she was surprised it had come from her own mouth.

"I hope you don't mind," Shawn said.

"Mind?" Reese replied, burying her head in his chest.

"I've been wanting to do this for a long time."

"Really? We haven't known each other for a long time."

"It feels like it, Reese."

He was stroking her hair. Saying her name. *Hers.*

The others, the celebrities, were watching from the wall. But they were somewhere else, and she was here.

And this was real.

As real as it got.

15

"OH, DEAR . . ." MR. LITTLE SAID, RUNNING INTO THE outer office with a plastic knife in his hand during the Monday rehearsal. "These do not retract. We were supposed to get *retractable* knives. To look like switchblades. We need them for this afternoon to rehearse the rumble scene. Darling, could I trouble you to go to Bardsley's Joke Shop and exchange them?"

Brianna turned from her computer screen. "Sure. How do I get there?"

"I was afraid you would ask that," Mr. Little said. "I know by instinct, but I'm directionally challenged." He smiled slyly. "Reginald knows. Let him drive. You won't mind that, will you?"

It took a second for her to realize he meant Steve. The

innuendo was a little easier to figure out. She took the knife and ran into the theater.

Steve was in the corridor, halfway around the theater to her left, arguing with Casey: "If the Jets enter at twelve o'clock, why do you have the interns running down that aisle with the props? You're making a logjam, Casey!"

"What's up?" Brianna said. Steve was intent on Casey's clipboard, so Brianna took a peek. On it was a copy of the theater's seating plan, carefully marked where all the entrances and exits occurred. The ramps were labeled like hands of the clock: twelve, two, four, etc.:

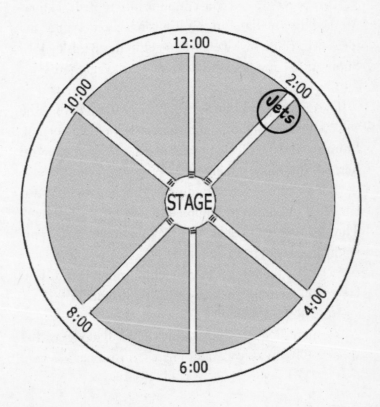

"See here?" Casey said to Steve, pointing to her clear, careful handwriting around the circumference. "I have the Jets in at two o'clock. I wrote it down."

"Mr. Bunt changed it," Steve retorted. "Didn't you hear him?"

"Yes," Casey said, nodding patiently. "But Mr. Bishop changed it back. You can see where I erased it."

"I just talked to Mr. Bunt about this, Casey," Steve said. "It's been changed again."

"Fine," Casey replied diplomatically. "I'll check with him."

"Um, Steve? I need you," Brianna interrupted. "I know. All the girls say that. But this is business, so don't get any ideas. Mr. Little says we have to get to the Bardsley Joke Shop, ASAP, and he says you know how to get there—"

"Owwww!"

The cry stopped Brianna in her tracks. It was Reese. She was on the floor of the eight-o'clock aisle, holding her foot. From around the theater, other actors were racing toward her, but Brianna got there first. "What happened?"

"I don't know!" Reese said, clutching her ankle. "I was late. The interns were supposed to give me my shoes . . . The shoes weren't ready . . . I took them anyway . . . my leg just went out from under me—"

Steve was there now, too, kneeling, along with Casey. He gently examined Reese's foot. "Twisted an ankle?"

"Yes!" Reese nodded. "I slipped on the—"

"Cement," Steve said, staring at the bottoms of her shoes. "Of course you did. There's no rubber on your soles." He called up the aisle. "*Who's supposed to rubberize the soles?*"

"I am!" called an intern from the back of the house. "But she grabbed the shoes away from me."

"That's no excuse, dude," Steve shouted, shaking his head disgustedly. "You know these shoes come from the shop with bare leather soles—and it's our job to fix them before anyone wears them. We need an ice pack, like now!" He put Reese's foot up on the next seat. "It doesn't look like it's swelling. Maybe just a sprain. The theater has a doctor on call. I'll call and make sure he sees you. Meanwhile keep it elevated. The ice will help."

"Thanks," Reese said, struggling to get up. "I'll be okay."

"Stay, don't make it worse," Casey admonished her.

Steve had his cell phone to his ear. "Hi, Steve Heller at the Sandy Shores Playhouse . . . yes, we need Dr. Lansdale . . . we have an injured ankle . . ."

Moments later, Reese's ankle was on ice, and Steve and Brianna got up to go. Steve stopped abruptly. "Before we leave," he said, "let me tell Callie, in case we get back late. She's my backup."

Brianna looked at Casey. "What about—?"

But Steve was gone.

"I don't believe he did that," Brianna said. "*You're* his other ASM."

"Well, I'm not surprised," Casey said, her shoulders slumped. "It's like I don't exist. Unless I make a mistake. Then he's all over me."

"Oh, Casey . . ." Brianna put her arms around her friend. "He's sort of alpha dog. And a control freak. For him, it's all about the show. You can't take it personally."

"He and I are supposed to work together, Brianna. Since when is *Callie* the backup? She's sets."

"Steve just knows her better. He'll warm up to you, Case."

Casey looked at her curiously. "Are you sticking up for him, Brianna? This doesn't sound like you."

Before she could think of an answer, Steve popped his head back into the theater. "Okay, let's go!"

Brianna gave Casey a squeeze and followed him out.

The sun scorched, bouncing waves of heat against the parking-lot blacktop. Steve walked fast, a step and a half ahead of her. From the back, she could see how each step bounced a little, how his feet turned out just a bit, like a dancer.

Their little—what was it, an "incident," a thing?—had stayed in her mind, like the chilly hint of winter on an April day. She wasn't sure what to think of it. And he hadn't exactly been quick to follow through. He hadn't said a word. A charter member of the Guys Say Nothing Club, along with Harrison.

Brianna took a sip from a water bottle as Steve opened the passenger door of an old red Mustang. "It's a disaster," he said, reaching in to toss stray paper bags and soda cans from the front seat to the back. "Sorry."

"I don't mind the car," Brianna replied, sliding into the seat in such a way that her legs did not make contact with the hot vinyl. "It's the heat that sucks."

The car gave a cough and a roar as Steve started it. He flicked on the air-conditioning, and a blast of dusty hot air hit Brianna in the face. "Sorry," he said, peeling out of the parking lot and onto Good Hope Road.

They drove in silence for a while, Brianna feeling scalded on the back of her legs every time they hit a pothole. He was driving too fast, and he should have parked in the shade to begin with. "You know, it wouldn't kill you to be nicer to Casey," she said irritably.

To her surprise, Steve nodded. "Yeah, I get impatient with . . . you know . . ." His voice trailed off.

"I don't know. Tell me."

"That . . . type."

"You get impatient with *Asian people?*"

"No!" Steve shifted uncomfortably in his seat. "You know . . . overprivileged, studious, rigid . . ."

Brianna tapped her fingers on the armrest. "*I'm* overprivileged, Steve. Casey's not. Her mom's a nurse and her dad left the family."

"She's always taking notes, writing down every little thing. Drives me crazy."

"What's wrong with doing that?"

He shrugged. "If you do too much of it, you miss the big picture. Theater's fast. Everybody's always changing their minds. After a while you have to just start trapping things in your head, on the fly. It's like the actors. Sometimes they only get one chance to do the blocking for a scene. There just isn't enough time for more. Actors are always afraid when they do summer stock for the first time. But soon they're keeping so much in their heads—entrances, exits, blocking, lines, choreography, harmonies—you have to do that to keep up."

"Casey's doing this for the first time. Don't be such a hard-ass. Not everyone's perfect like you."

"Yeah . . ." He sighed. "I should ease up . . ."

By the time they pulled into a small parking lot, near a Wendy's and a Trader Joe's, the car was nice and cool. Just up the block, in an old clapboard building, was Bardsley's Joke Shop. When they opened the door, a raucous recorded laugh bellowed in their ears. "The doorbell," Steve explained. Holding up the rigid plastic knives they needed to return, he called out, "Hey, Howard, what are you trying to do, kill our lead actors?"

Behind the counter sat a balding man with a plaid shirt and grim expression, watching a tiny-screen TV. "Hope springs eternal," he said. Halfheartedly, he pushed a small box of spring-loaded retractable rubber knives toward them.

Brianna examined them quickly and said, "We'll take them." Then she and Steve made the trade and said good-bye. The quicker the better. The place smelled like a three-day-old ham sandwich.

The car was still cool when they got back in. Steve turned on the ignition and opened the box, testing the knives. "Perfect."

"I think Howard's ready to retire," Brianna remarked.

Reaching for the gearshift, Steve laughed. "I'll tell him you said so."

"Aha! I got you to laugh. I never heard you laugh."

"It's been tough since I escaped Bedlam." He shifted into reverse.

"Bedlam . . ." Brianna thought a moment, then held up a plastic knife. "But at last, your arm—"

"—is complete again!" Steve howled. *Sweeney Todd!* Yo, you are *good!*"

"But . . . how do *you* know that?"

"You're not the only actor in this car," Steve said.

"I thought you were—"

"A stage manager?" Steve laughed. "Only because I wasn't allowed to audition. I'm totally hard-core, baby. Heading to Juilliard, Yale, Carnegie-Mellon—whoever takes me—and then watch out, Broadway."

He was serious. As serious as she was. She tried to put herself in his shoes—and suddenly all his anger made sense. "So . . . all this rage against the Ridgeport kids—it's really personal for you."

"Think about it," he said, his voice soft and thoughtful. "Ever since this theater started, kids from our school have interned every summer but never been allowed to act. Then your parents give a party, your mom suggests that you guys fill the open roles—and next thing, you're all auditioning. And no one even asks us."

"Yeah," Brianna said, letting his words sink in. All her life, her mom and dad had drummed into her head the Glaser family motto—*From whom much is given, much is expected.* A Glaser was never supposed to use wealth to an unfair advantage. A Glaser always remembered the family's modest beginnings, always gave back, always thought of others first. Wealth was power, and power could make you step on people—and sometimes you didn't even realize it. "I'm sorry, Steve. You guys got a raw deal. I didn't realize—none of us did."

"Not your fault." Steve shot her a rueful grin. "Hey, which of us would have said no if *our* parents had pulled strings, huh? We shouldn't go blaming you for what your mom did."

He released the clutch and the car lurched backward.

"Whoa . . . easy," Brianna said with a challenging smile. "There's a law against attempted murder, even in Baltimore."

Steve paused, halfway out of the parking space. "Wait. *Kiss Me, Kate?*"

"Not Kate. Brianna. And don't mind if I do."

She grabbed his head and planted a kiss on his cheek. An old joke. She had pulled it on Harrison a thousand times when they were in middle school—every time he mentioned the title of that play. It always sent him screaming from the room.

Steve turned, with a startled expression she had never seen, as if he had just traded in new, bigger facial features for the old ones. The car stalled, the engine died, and behind them a waiting SUV sounded an angry horn blast. But Brianna heard only the sound of the creaking driver's seat as he leaned over to her, saw only the question in his eyes.

She didn't know why she had done that. She didn't know why she had done half the crazy things she'd done in her life. But she knew the answer to his question.

As her eyes closed, and she felt the surprising coolness of his lips, she tried to fight back the obvious thought, that if anyone had told her she would be here right now, in the parking lot of Bardsley's Joke Shop, kissing Reginald Stephens Heller, and *liking* it, she would have cackled with laughter.

But they hadn't. And she was. And she did.

A lot.

June 29, 08:48 P.M.
changchangchang: *i feel like quitting, bri.*
changchangchang: *i will never get along with steve.*
dramakween: don't, casey. i beat him up for u. he admits he was being impatient.
changchangchang: *he was being a jerk.*
changchangchang: *i can't do it. i can't just memorize everything. that's not the way i work. or the way anyone should work.*
dramakween: case, people have to move fast in summer stock.
changchangchang: *i move fast. but i keep a record. a record is important.*
dramakween: so is getting along with your coworkers!
changchangchang: *why ru on his side?*
dramakween: im not! im just trying to broker a peace.
dramakween: u guys are like the mideast.
dramakween: look, hes going to try harder.

dramakween: ul see.

changchangchang: bri, if u start hooking up with him, i will kick & scream.

dramakween: u have an active imagination. hey, can u believe reese's ankle? 1 minute she's dying, the next she's up there doing the mambo in an ace bandage.

changchangchang: ur changing the subject.

dramakween: i assure you im not going to get married todayyyyyyyy.

changchangchang: that's a line from a show . . . is it "company"?

dramakween: U GOOGLED IT!!! Not fair!!!

changchangchang has signed off.

Part 2
A Boy Like That

July 8

16

"BREAK A LEG!" REESE SAID, BARGING INTO SHAWN'S dressing room.

She couldn't believe it was opening night. Gah! It hadn't seemed like *two weeks*.

It was going to be hard to give up the role of Teresita, now that Marisol was coming back. Even though it was a small role, Reese loved it. And she was good at it. Both Mr. Bunt and Mr. Bishop had commented that Reese was one of the only people who hadn't seemed to be "phoning it in" during yesterday's dress rehearsal.

Along with Shawn. Of course. He was a pro.

Now he was standing up, his eyes on her as he adjusted his shirt. She quickly kicked the door shut, threw her arms around him, and wrapped her right leg around his waist.

As she gave him a long, deep kiss, she wrapped her left leg around him, lifting herself completely off the floor. "And break another leg . . . and—"

"Uh, let's stop right there," Shawn said with a laugh.

Reese sighed, slowly sliding off. He was smiling at her now, a tiny bit of makeup on his face to accentuate the bones—as if he needed it—and a tight white T-shirt over baggy jeans. His table was crammed with bouquets, boxes of chocolates, handwritten notes for opening night.

He was opening tonight.

She wasn't.

It hurt. It was the first public performance of the show, the first time it counted. And the first time she would *not* be dancing the role of Teresita. Marisol would be back, everything would be normal again. No reviewer would discover her. Swings were not discovered.

She grinned at Shawn. *He* didn't care. He still knew who she was, what she could do. As long as he was in her life, she could deal.

"You look hot," Reese said.

"You look scalding," Shawn replied.

She adjusted her tight tank top ever so slightly. After a week of sneaking around, "running lines" in this room, she knew what he liked. "I *hope* I don't distract you when you're singing about Marisol."

"Ow. I'll wear sunglasses." Shawn laughed. "Hey, is Marisol here? She's been gone so long I almost forgot what she looks like."

"I can't believe she's going to do this—pop in on opening night," Reese said. "That is so—" She held her tongue. No use being bitter. This was what everyone knew would happen.

A soft *tap-tap-tap* sounded at the door.

"Come in!" Shawn called.

"It's been a long absence," Reese continued. "Not that it matters, but isn't there a rule about this—like, in the actors' union?"

Shawn shrugged. "Stuart's been sending her MP3s of the rehearsals. He thinks she can handle it. She's done the role before. I talked to her a couple of nights ago. She was bummed they weren't going to take the pilot, but she was excited to be coming back."

Reese looked at her watch. It was nearly half hour. "Well, rehearsing with you was . . . fun . . ." She reached up and threaded her arms through his, reaching around his back . . .

TAP-TAP-TAP.

"*Come in!*" she shouted, quickly pulling away.

The door opened slowly and Casey peered in, looking shell-shocked. "Um, hi . . . ?"

Before she could continue, Steve barged in behind her. "Reese, what are you doing?" he demanded.

"Getting naked with Shawn and Casey—it's a Ridgeport High School tradition on opening night," Reese said. "Want to join us?"

"Where's your costume?" he barged on.

"Uh . . . well, on Lacey, I'd guess. Since that's where it belongs, considering it is her costume, and she is about to go onstage."

Steve whirled on Casey. "I sent Casey to tell you, didn't she tell you?"

"I was about to," Casey said, then quickly turned toward Reese. "Lacey is playing Maria, just like in rehearsals. Marisol's not coming back. The network changed their minds. They're ordering more episodes and she's broken her contract with us."

"*Whaaat?*" Reese said.

Shawn punched his fist in the air. "*Awesome!* I mean, for her. It's a good break . . ."

She was not hearing this. This could not be true. This was a joke.

"This isn't real, right?" Reese said suspiciously, glancing from Casey to Steve. "If you're screwing around with me Steve, I swear I will become your worst nightmare—"

"It's real," Steve said, "so deal with it, okay? Because *we have a show to do!*"

"But—how can I—what about the costume—didn't they take it out?" Reese said.

"Yes," Steve said, "but there's this adjustable panel or something—"

"And *whoooooose* idea was that, thank you very much?" shouted Charles, peeking in. "Break a leg, my hot little *estrella!*"

"Charles . . . ?"

He was smiling. Like his face had some strange inner light. Like the farmhands hunched over Dorothy's bed at the end of *The Wizard of Oz.* The trusty farmhands who were full of love and happiness.

Who would never, *ever* lie.

"Oh . . . my . . ." It was real. She knew it by looking at Charles. "GeeeaaaAAAAHHHHH! "

Now Shawn was lifting her off her feet, laughing—and she could see Steve's face, turning away . . . Casey, smiling and tearful . . . Charles, looking like a proud papa. "Pinch me!" she screamed. "Pinch—*ow!*"

It hurt. Shawn's pinch hurt. *In tonight's performance, the role of Teresita will be played by Reese Van Cleve!* "It's my debut!" She hopped down and hugged Casey, then Charles. "Oh, I love you both!"

"We'll say we knew you when," Charles said, stepping back and twirling to show off his costume—tight T-shirt, a red bandanna around his neck, and jeans that accentuated a bit too much of his ample waistline. "So . . . enough about you. How do *I* look? Don't answer. This is why slimming leather jackets were invented, and I'm about to fetch mine."

"Why are *you* in costume?" Steve asked.

"My boy, you *don't* think the Charlushers would be seen in public in basic black?" Charles replied, leaving the room with a little back kick. "Toodles! Break a leg, Jets and Sharks!"

"*Half-hour!*" Ms. Richards's voice called out from behind Steve. "*Get in your costumes and report to the Green Room for a meeting with Mr. Little!*"

"Meeting?" Steve said in disbelief, throwing up his hands. "We're already at half hour, dress rehearsal was a disaster, Bunt is still working on the knife fight with José, Bishop's on a conference call with the theater's lawyer and Marisol's agent, we're almost sold out, there's a line out the door, and the box-office computer is down—"

"We're sold out?" Reese said.

"Yes, which means get into your costume now so you don't look like THAT in front of paying customers!"

Thwap. Right back to reality. Good old Steve.

As he stormed out, disappearing into a rush of black-clad interns, Casey sighed. "Did he really say that to you, in that tone of voice, on the day of your professional debut?"

"No prob," Reese said with a cheerful smile. "I'll wait till the intermission. And then I will remove my stiletto heels and impale him."

"Give me your other shoe," Casey said. "I'll get him where the sun don't shine."

"Casey!" Reese said in utter shock.

"Sorry! Sorry . . ." Casey's face was a deep red, as if she couldn't believe what she had said. And when a laugh escaped Reese's mouth in an unsightly spray, Casey couldn't help but join in.

Shawn shook his head. "I will never understand chicks."

Reese wanted desperately to give him a kiss, but not with Casey standing there, so she settled for a hug from behind and ran toward the dressing room.

Steve and Brianna were standing by the tent, staring moonily into each other's eyes and laughing. *Oh, please,* Reese thought with a silent mental groan. They were slipping. They had been trying to keep their little something a secret. She knew. Charles did, too.

Not that there was anything wrong with it—but *Steve*? Brianna must have been really lonely. She could do better than that cockroach.

As she headed into the dressing room, the other Jet and Shark girls were heading out. Her costume had been draped over the chair, and a small light blue Tiffany box was sitting on her makeup table.

She carefully untied the ribbon and opened the lid. It was a sterling-silver pin, with the letters *SSP* crossed diagonally with the letters *WSS*. "*West Side Story . . .* Sandy Shores Playhouse," she murmured.

Reese turned to see Lacey, all made up as Maria. Her hair and eyebrows had been darkened, her light skin bronzed with makeup, her lips a deep shade of red. "It's from Mr. Little," she said. "Isn't it beautiful?"

"*You're* beautiful," Reese replied.

"I'm nervous." Lacey leaned down to give Reese a hug. "Come on, let me help you out."

Lacey quickly helped Reese do her makeup, and Reese changed into her costume. It was a little stiff-looking, until Reese pulled down one shoulder. "Hot?" Reese said.

"Ay-yi-yi!" Lacey replied. "Let's go, *chica*."

They raced to the Green Room, which was throbbing with noise. Casey, Harrison, and Brianna immediately smothered Reese with screams and hugs. In the corner a group of Jets wrestled with the harmony to "The Quintet" while three Sharks tried valiantly to butch up their jetés. Sue Van Cott, one of the Jets girls, was blasting a high note that surely had the neighborhood dogs howling, and everyone else was generally yacking, squealing, stretching, laughing, or vocalizing.

"ATTENTION PLEASE!" Mr. Bishop's voice cut through the noise. "EVERYONE IN SEATS!"

The cast scrambled into folding chairs. Shawn was sitting on the edge of a table, smiling easily as if this kind of thing happened to him every day. He gave Reese a confident thumbs-up.

Mr. Bishop, flanked by a smiling Mr. Little, an exhausted Mr. Bunt, and a confident-looking Mr. Fredericks, leaned on the rehearsal piano and waited for silence. "Cast," he finally said in a soft but firm voice, "we have been through a lot this week. We lost one of our leads to Hollywood, but gained a lot of new energy."

Reese beamed. He was talking about *her*, she knew it.

"I was just around front," Mr. Bishop continued, "and had to assign three of our high school interns to manage the waiting line for cancellations, which now stretches halfway down the parking lot."

A surge of excitement went through the cast. "Yyyyyessss!" shouted José, and the Sharks began slapping one another in an elaborate handshake developed for the show.

"Let's give it up for our star, Shawn Nolan, who is a large part of the cause of such popularity," Mr. Bishop said.

A loud cheer rang out, and as Shawn modestly waved them away, Reese watched their faces. They loved him. Everybody loved him.

And she had him.

"But let's not forget that it's the quality of the theater, the years of excellent productions built up in this community, that has kept *all* the houses full and *all* the productions first-class," Mr. Bishop went on, "so I want you to continue the tradition and all *GET OUT THERE AND RUMMMMMBLE!*"

"YEEAAAA!"

As everyone got up to leave, Steve appeared in the door, looking frantic. "Mr. Bishop . . ." he said.

"Ah, Steve—you can tell Ms. Richards to let in the house now," Mr. Bishop said.

"We have to delay the opening," Steve insisted, gesturing over his shoulder. "Look . . ."

Mr. Bishop and the others rushed to the door, the cast falling in behind them.

Outside the theater's rear entrance stood the ushers, in two lines. The guys were identically dressed in leather jackets, T-shirts, rolled-up jeans, and high-top sneakers. The women were wearing tight ruffled party dresses and fifties hairdos. Their average age looked to be about sixty-five.

"Now, darlin's," Charles was saying. "When you hand out the programs, I want to see a little style . . . like this . . ." He licked his right index finger, pressed it to his hip, and bounced it off with a "Tssss!" while handing out a program with his other hand.

One by one, the "girls" tried the technique.

Reese howled. She could see Harrison, Casey, and Brianna convulsing just inside the door.

"This isn't funny!" Steve said. "We can't let them go out there like this! We're a professional—"

"CHARLES!" Mr. Bishop called out in a grim, booming voice, striding purposefully across the walkway toward the ushers.

"Oh!" Charles said uncertainly. "Hi, Mr. B. We were just . . ."

His voice faded as Mr. Bishop stood towering over him, his arms on his hips. "In all my years in the theater, I have *never* seen anyone do something like this."

"Really?" Charles was trembling. "I—well, I just thought . . . as a thematic . . . thing . . ."

"I was wondering," Mr. Bishop said, placing an arm on Charles's shoulder. "Do you think they could do a little mambo as they walk down the aisle?"

17

THE LIGHTS DIMMED AND THE MUSIC BEGAN.

Reese felt petrified.

Numb.

Freezing cold.

Exhilarated.

As she huddled in the shadows next to Harrison at the back of the theater, listening to the overture and watching the late theatergoers scurry in the darkness to their seats, she had to hug herself to keep from shivering. Was *this* what it was like? Was this what you felt every night in professional theater?

The theater had cooled off since the afternoon, with a salty sea breeze whipping through the open tent flaps. The spotlight was on Mr. Fredericks, dressed in a

Hawaiian shirt and linen pants and swinging his body as he conducted the opening notes. There were about ten instruments, but it sounded like a huge concert jazz band. The place was packed—most of them unfamiliar faces but a healthy showing of Ridgeport people, too, including the Glasers; the Van Cleves; Mr. Levin, the Drama Club faculty adviser; and Ms. Gunderson, the DC's music supervisor.

A few late-minute stragglers, led quickly down the ramps by the stylish Charlushers, took their seats, filling in the few empty canvas chairs that ringed the stage.

"Why does this feel so scary?" Reese whispered.

"Because they're strangers," Harrison said with a smile. "And they're paying money to see professionals."

"Aren't *you* scared?" Reese asked.

"Not enough time to be scared." As Mr. Fredericks stabbed his baton into the air for the final crashing chords, Harrison crouched and got ready to enter. All over the theater, the Jets raced down the other ramps, a sudden attack from all sides. The stage suddenly exploded with light, and there they were—in the back-alley slums of New York City's decrepit West Side, dancing tough, all angles and finger snaps and sudden jagged movement, to the brassy jazz riffs from the orchestra.

"It's magic time," came a soft but heavily Puerto Rican–accented voice in her ear as José passed her, clapping Harrison on the shoulder—and then both guys suddenly took off at a sprint, down the six-o'clock ramp and onto the stage, to begin the Shark attack on Jet turf.

Reese stood rooted to the spot, transfixed. When she

felt an arm resting on her shoulder, she knew from the touch it was Shawn. "'Sup?" he whispered into her ear.

"So far, so good," she said.

"This is your night, Reese." He was smiling, his face lit dimly by the reflected light from the stage. "It doesn't get better than this."

Brianna's eyes followed Reese as she danced on the stage, her smile sassy, her eyes never showing an ounce of fear. She had grown so. Her over-the-top show-offy style was just right for her chorus role. You couldn't take your eyes off her.

The whole show was nearly perfect. Harrison was powerful, even in his small role. Lacey was a beautiful Maria with a voice that rang the rafters. And Shawn—well, a star was a star.

She could only take about two and a half scenes before leaving the theater.

It was a sharp pain, not even subtle. It gripped her whole body, turning her inside out. It was impossible to watch and not feel it, not feel that she belonged up there, too. It never really did go away. When you had theater in your blood, it always hit you. It was there for life.

Darting outside, she took a few deep breaths. Shawn was singing "Maria" now, alone onstage. Near the dressing room, Harrison was playing Hacky Sack with two of the other actors, all of them dressed in fifties garb. Two worlds. Brianna slipped away to the office and sat on her chair. The show was being piped into the office via speakers—there was no escaping it. On her monitor was a pink Post-it note—*Brianna, pls. help the caterers when they arrive for the cast party*—which she pulled off, folded the gluey part in on itself, and jammed in her pocket. She glanced at the e-mail in-box, which was full of good-luck messages to Mr. Little. She got a shiver reading some of the names in the "from" lines—Victor Garber, Billy Crudup, Kristin Chenoweth—Broadway stars who had worked with Mr. Little before.

As actors, she thought. *Not glorified gofers.*

With a sigh, she shuffled back outside. A group of interns was setting up the Green Room for the party. Steve had come in from the show and was with them, directing the placement of tables. The song "America" blared through the monitor.

"Couldn't watch, huh?" he said. "Me either. It's hard not to be up there."

Brianna smiled. Yeah. He knew.

Suddenly Harrison's voice called out, "*Hey, Bri!* The gang war-council scene is next—come and watch!"

"We'll go together," Steve whispered. "Keep ourselves strong."

"*Excuse me*," a voice shouted, and Brianna felt herself bumped from behind as Callie barged past her, carrying a tray with plastic glasses glued onto it, and a couple of fake ice cream sundaes.

"Are you sure you want to be seen with me?" Brianna asked Steve. "There goes your street cred with your peeps."

"God, this is so Tony and Maria," Steve said. "Okay, you go first. I'll sneak in shortly. But I weel be quiet so Bernardo does not hearrr."

"*Te adoro*, Stevie," Brianna said in an earthy whisper.

"It's *Esteban*," he said.

Harrison was running into the theater with the other Sharks and Jets. Brianna jogged in after him and stood in the back. The stage was dark, and as the scenery rolled in, Callie and her interns were placing props on all the surfaces. There was a loud thump, a couple of muttered curses, but when the lights went up—voilà—the Jets were in a really cool set designed to look like Doc's drugstore. This was the Jets' "war meeting" to discuss their fight with the Sharks.

As Harrison and the Sharks entered, upping the tension, Steve sneaked in behind Brianna. He was squinting at the stage. "What the heck is that?" he said, pointing to a lump on the floor by the ten-o'clock ramp.

"A bar stool?" she guessed. "Maybe one of the interns dropped it?"

And now the Sharks were making their exit, chased away by the cop character, Lieutenant Shrank—toward the ten-o'clock ramp—led by Harrison.

As Harrison ran right into the stool, Brianna flinched. There was a collective gasp from the audience on that side as his foot connected. He fell over the stool, nearly tumbled into the first row of seats, and managed to clomp down into the ramp.

In a moment he was sprinting up the aisle. Steve and Brianna ran around the top of the seats to join him. Mr.

Bunt was already at the top of the aisle, looking at Harrison with concern. "Are you okay?" they all whispered.

"Who left that there?" Harrison demanded, leaning over to hold his ankle. "I almost got killed."

As he stormed away, Callie stepped forward from the shadows. "Sorry," she said timidly.

"Well, you'd better go explain to *him*," Brianna said, glancing out the door.

Callie looked incredulous, as if apologizing to Steve was enough.

Steve nodded and Callie slumped out of the theater. Brianna watched as she caught up to Harrison just outside the dressing room. He did not look happy.

"There goes my street cred," said Steve.

18

SHE'D DONE IT. AS SHE STOOD IN THE CORRIDOR behind the last row of seats, watching the final scene, her heart pounded ridiculously.

Reese could barely remember what had happened, it had all been so fast. But the steps had been there. The lines, too. Even most of the harmonies. And now the show was ending.

Muted, mournful trumpets rang through the theater now. A death knell. In the spotlight, Tony's—Shawn's—body was lifted onto the shoulders of the Jets. Such a sad scene—the last confrontation between the Sharks and Jets, after Tony had been shot with a bullet to the back.

As Charles sidled up to her, shoulder to shoulder, Reese choked back a tear.

"Oh. This part *always* gets me," whispered Charles.

And then the procession—Jets and Sharks—slowly climbed the eight-o'clock ramp. As the last drumbeat sounded, the house faded to black.

The applause began almost immediately. When the procession reached the top of the ramp and moved into the darkened rear corridor near Reese, Shawn quickly climbed down. The Jets raced around the theater to the opposite side. Reese felt someone grabbing her hand and turned to see Casey, looking just as excited as she was. When she spotted the Jets at the other side, she pushed Reese forward and shouted "Go—*ensemble . . . go!*"

Reese raced in with the Sharks from the eight-o'clock aisle, as the Jets ran in from two-o'clock. They met in the center, scowled at one another, and then joined hands, smiling at the crowd and taking their bows. Reese could barely hear the noise. She was watching the faces—tearful, beaming. She spotted her mom and dad in the fifth row and blew them a kiss. As she ran to the lip of the stage with the rest of the chorus, she made sure to grab Harrison's butt for old time's sake, and he shook his finger at her as they knelt, letting the leads race in for their bows.

Shawn, of course, came in last.

And of course, the place went berserk. Roses flew onto the stage, as well as a few pieces of underwear and a Frisbee with WILL YOU MARRY ME? printed on it. Reese felt a tap on her shoulder and turned to see a little old lady hand her a small paper plate of homemade chocolate-chip cookies. "From my granddaughter," she said proudly. "Give it to the young man, would you? It's from Rebecca. Rebecca *Turnbull*. That's T-U-R . . ."

Reese could barely hear the old lady for the shrieking,

and Shawn stood grinning at the audience, soaking up the sound and the light.

"Partyyy!" someone shouted, and the cast broke for the six-o'clock exit before the house lights went on.

Outside, in front of the dressing room, Charles was waiting. "Group hug!" he screamed.

He, Reese, Harrison, and Brianna all jumped in together. "You were soooo awesome!" Reese said to Harrison.

"So were you," Harrison replied.

"And my Charlushers?" Charles asked.

"*Fabulous!*" they all shouted together.

"I have to change out of this sweaty thing," Reese said. "See you at the party in the Green Room?"

"You'll see Harrison," Charles said. "It's a cast party. The interns are having chips and soda in the scene shop."

"Oh, please," Reese said. "You can sneak in. They can't let us in without letting you. Brianna and Casey, too."

"The Sandy Shores interns will love that," Charles said.

"Tell them to crash the party, too," Reese said. "And the Charlushers."

Shawn was emerging backward from the theater now, nodding to fans who were trying to follow him out. Five or six of the biggest interns, including Marc, were holding them back.

Shawn finally bounded free as the cast enfolded him in an embrace—screaming, piling on, like the last game of the World Series.

They congratulated one another, cried, vowed this was the best show *ever*—all of it so cozily familiar to Reese. It was just like RHS. Jaded professionals or not, it was the same.

Then they all raced into the dressing rooms, changed, and headed for the cast party in the Green Room.

Already the speakers were blaring, a DJ bouncing to the music against the far wall.

"EEEEEE!" Reese shouted, cornering Shawn alone, throwing her arms around him as he lifted her off the floor and swung her around.

"Damn, you looked good," he said. "You distracted me in the gym scene. Almost forgot my dance steps."

"But you're pledged to Maria," Reese replied coyly.

"You better believe it," said Lacey, dancing past them with Charles, who blew them both a kiss.

As Charles pulled Lacey into a line dance being started by members of the Charlushers, Reese noticed the brooch on Lacey's jacket. "Oops, forgot something," she said to Shawn, racing out of the Green Room and into the dressing room.

She nearly collided with Lauren, who was picking costumes off the floor. "Sorry!" Reese said, rushing to her table. She opened the box and took out the brooch, staring into the mirror as she pinned it on.

In here, the music from the cast party was nothing more than a muffled bass line. Snippets of conversation between the lighting and set designers, Mr. Fibich and Mr. Sainte, occasionally blared from the speakers on the wall, which piped in the sound from the stage. Behind Reese, several interns were putting clothes into wicker baskets. One girl was pushing a broom, while a guy across the room complained about a half-eaten Subway veggie delight that had leaked all over a dance outfit.

"Nice," Lauren said, noticing Reese's brooch in the mirror. "Where'd you get it?"

"Mr. Little gave it to"—Reese's words choked in her throat—". . . us."

Lauren paused and looked away. "Oh. Well, have a nice time at the *cast* party," she said.

"Listen, you guys should just come by—" Reese began.

But Lauren had rushed out.

With a sigh, Reese raced back to the Green Room. The line dance had gone viral, and now most of the cast was mixing it up with the Charlushers. Reese looked around for Shawn and saw him next to the DJ, bent-kneed with one foot against the wall behind him, signing programs for a few of the chorus girls.

"Let's dance," she said, cozying up to him.

Shawn finished up the signing, thanked the girls, grabbed Reese by the hand, and dragged her to the floor. The DJ was spinning an old Four Seasons song. Shawn could dance a killer jitterbug. Reese was flying over his back, through his legs, spinning in the air around his forearm. Before long the dance floor had cleared and everyone—the cast, the staff, Mr. Little, Mr. Bunt, Ms. Richards, and Mr. Bishop—had formed a wide ring around them, cheering them on.

At the end of the song, they did a spectacular dip that Reese turned into a full split—to a roar of applause.

They fell into each other's arms, waving at the crowd and laughing. "Let's go," he whispered into her ear.

"Go?"

"Somewhere else. Alone."

"Alone?"

"Are you going to repeat everything I say?"

Reese swallowed. "No! I mean, yes! I mean—"

"It's just crowded in here," Shawn said. "I don't want to sign programs and dance with every person. I need air and quiet."

"Where?" Reese asked.

He shrugged. "You're the one who knows the neighborhood."

"Um . . . Elsa's on the Park?" Reese said. "It's a sidewalk café in Ridgeport, not too far from the beach. I'm starving."

"Deal."

They sneaked out of the party and into Shawn's car, reaching Elsa's in minutes. As usual, it was packed— but Reese knew the owners, who *loved* to be known as a celebrity hang, and a table mysteriously appeared in a corner of the sidewalk café.

Shawn put on his sunglasses even though it was dark. "I'll have a pizza with pineapple," he said.

"That is the grossest thing I ever heard," said Reese.

Shawn's eyes widened. "You have never been to the West Coast, have you?"

"I've been to New Jersey. Once," Reese said. "That's west."

Laughing, Shawn pulled a packet of Equal from its holder and threw it at her.

Click.

A clutch of giggling middle school girls had taken

a photo. "Can you . . ." one of them said. "Oh, never mind . . . but could you . . . ?"

Before Reese knew it, she was being handed a camera, and she shot a photo of Shawn with his new friends.

As the waiter served the pineapple pizza, a group of Reese's classmates—nerdy Kate Knoblauch and her buds from the math team—came bounding over. "Ohmygodohmygodohmygod! Oh! My! God! Reese, that can't really be like *Shawn Nolan*?"

Shawn took off his sunglasses. "It could be."

"AAAAAAAAAAAAAAAAAA!" shouted Anne Grimly and Alyssa Murchison.

"Could you sign, um . . ." Kate looked around for something to sign but finally held out her arm. "Here?"

She watched Shawn as he gave the girls his best head-shot smile.

The girls gaped at every movement he made as he signed his name on two forearms, the back of a hand, and a napkin stained with carrot cake.

As the girls glided, giggling, back to their seats, Reese looked down and realized that she had been tracing her own name with her nail on the napkin on the table in front of her.

Reese Van Cleve, Reese Van Cleve, Reese . . .

Shawn broke her out of her fantasy: "Um, you want to go to the beach?"

"Sure," she said.

Shawn slapped a hundred-dollar bill on the table and stood up.

"You—that's—but we didn't even have—" Reese stammered.

"I do it all the time," Shawn said. "People appreciate it. You'd be amazed."

"Thank you!" the waiter said incredulously.

"No problem at all," Reese said over her shoulder, following Shawn out the door.

19

"AND *TURN* . . ." CHARLES CALLED OUT, CAUSING some of the Charlushers to turn right, others to turn left, and the rest to attempt a full spin, scattering other dancers like bowling pins. He had succeeded in drawing almost the whole cast party into the dance.

Brianna tried to keep from laughing. She became aware of a buzz in her pants pocket, and pulled out her cell phone to see a text message:

IS THERE A PLACE FOR US?

The title from a WSS song, turned into a question. The return phone number was Steve's. She looked quickly around the room. He was standing just outside the Green Room door, an innocent look on his face.

She typed back

U CAN DO BETTER THAN THAT . . .

Dancing over toward Steve, she caught him just as he saw the message. "Hey, I meant it," he said. "Want to get out of here?"

"The party's just getting started," Brianna said.

"For you, maybe," he replied. "We're not invited."

"Of course you are," Brianna said. "Just come on in."

Steve shook his head. "*You* can do that. Your friends and the friends of anyone with the last name Glaser. Otherwise it's a cast party. They make it clear to us in preseason. Fire laws. Overcrowding. Liability. Mr. Little has a separate party for the interns. Not like this, though. Ours is lame."

Brianna suddenly felt guilty. "So . . . what are you suggesting?"

"You read my message."

"You want to go somewhere else? With me? Your friends would kill you if they saw you leaving with the enemy."

"They don't have to see us." Steve glanced over his shoulder. "I'll be under the canopy in front of the theater in five minutes."

"And what if I don't show up?"

Steve smiled. "I'll look like an idiot."

Brianna danced back into the party. This was so undercover. So Jets-Sharks. Nonchalantly she made her way to the other side of the Green Room—and then, when no one was looking, out the rear door.

She sneaked around the back of the building, taking

care to walk outside the shafts of light that shone from the open costume room and prop room doors. In the first, Lauren was silently sorting clothes with interns, and in the other Callie and another team were putting props back on shelves. A few other interns were eating chips and listening silently to iPods in the scene shop.

Brianna felt a pang of sympathy. Well, at least she was not crashing the cast party anymore. Quickly she ran around the theater to the front. Steve was there, waiting.

"Did anyone see you?" he asked.

"I didn't hear any gunshots."

"Ha ha. My car or yours?"

"Mine . . . if it's not trashed," Brianna said.

Steve gave her a look. "I told you we didn't do that."

"God, you're so *serious*." They climbed into the car. "I feel like going to the beach."

"You read my mind," Steve said.

She didn't know if Steve liked Gwen Stefani, but that's who was blaring over her speakers as the car started. She lowered the window and let the music out to the world, and they sang along, winding their way through town and onto the highway.

The beach was already closed, but Brianna drove around the barricades and parked in a remote corner of the lot. As she turned off the engine, the music gave way to silence, punctuated by seagull squeals and the crash of the surf.

She climbed out of the car, closed the door, and stretched her arms to the star-freckled sky. Shutting her eyes, she took a deep breath, letting her lungs fill with the cool salty air.

Steve's arms surrounded her from behind, and she held them across her body for a moment, rocking back and forth. "Let's walk," she said, taking his hand.

They hurried through the lot and onto the walkway. Only a few cars dotted the parking lot, and if there were any people on the beach, they were well hidden. Brianna took off her shoes and began walking toward the surf, until the soft sand gave way to hard. She headed west, feeling the coolness between her toes. The day's weariness lifted with the muffled whoosh of each incoming wave.

In the distance, way out to sea, a red light blinked as it moved slowly across the horizon. They walked silently until the beach narrowed and the rolling sand dunes obscured the sight of the boardwalk and beach buildings. It felt like the end of the earth.

Brianna stopped, taking it all in. Steve wasn't looking at the light or the dunes or the stars above but at her face. His smile was as much a question as an invitation.

"How do you do that?" she asked. "That question-y thing with your face? It's like you're nine years old."

"I was trying for eight," Steve replied.

"No, you weren't." Brianna grinned. "You know, I used to hate you. Some of my friends still do."

Steve laughed. "You got over it. Maybe they will, too."

"Then I better hurry," Brianna said, "before I have competition."

And without a word, without a signal, they were walking

into the dunes, over a crest and around a waving patch of beach grass—into a valley with a gentle slope like giant open arms.

Brianna sank to her knees. Steve was laying his jacket out like a blanket, taking off his shirt and laying that out, too, and Brianna couldn't wait for any more, so she pulled him down, kissing him deeply, breathing him in like the air. And it all seemed to blow away—the sand, the beach, the sky—leaving only the warmth of lips and hands, the sweet tangle of limbs, the feel of his chest, the touches that asked with tenderness and then proceeded, always knowing, always hearing yes.

Until his hold suddenly became rigid.

"Brianna? *Steve?*"

The voice was a pinprick, and Steve held Brianna close as she turned to see a familiar silhouette peering above the next sand dune.

"Reese . . . ?" Brianna said. "What are you doing here?"

"Oh my God, I am *so* sorry," Reese said.

Another silhouette took shape next to her. "Dudes," said Shawn, giving a little wave. "Nice night."

20

July 9, 01:17 A.M.
dramakween: *that was, um, interesting . . .*
dancerslut: STEVE?????????????? UR DOING IT
WITH STEVE?
dramakween: *reese, u wont tell anyone, right?*
dancerslut: im not that stupid.
dramakween: *thank you.*
dancerslut: looks like we both have our dirty little
secrets.

The next day was cool and gray, as if the spring had
decided to knock Long Island on the head one last time
before finally giving in to summer. In her shoulder bag,
Brianna had the long-sleeved shirt Steve had lent her last

night. She thought about putting it on—trumpeting to the world what had happened, and screw 'em if they couldn't take a joke—but it was going to be a long season, and her pacifist sensibilities won out.

As she picked up her pace, hoping to warm up, she smiled. She had been smiling since the moment she'd wakened. The night was still in her, like the lingering taste of an almost-perfect dessert. Seeing Reese and Shawn had shot the mood. But now she and Steve had something to look forward to. An incentive to try again.

And again. And again.

It wasn't ten yet, but as she approached the theater she could already hear the piano plunking out dance tunes and the loud thumping of feet on the stage. Listening to dancers rehearse, without seeing them, was always strange. You'd think they were an angry but oddly rhythmic herd of buffalo.

As she rounded the building, she saw Casey bustling out of the costume room, cell phone in hand. "Sorry, I don't know where—oh, wait, here she comes. I'll tell her." She hung up the phone and called out, "Mr. L wants you now."

"Did he try to call me?" Brianna asked, suddenly realizing her cell was on vibrate and in her shoulder bag.

"Yes," Casey shot back. "Several times."

Brianna paused. Something wasn't right. "Casey? Are you okay?"

"I have a lot to do," Casey said, walking away.

"Ho-o-o-old on," Brianna said, following her. "What happened, Case?"

Casey whirled around. Her eyes were narrow, her face pinched. "It's all a big joke to you, isn't it?"

Brianna cocked her head. "What do you mean?"

"It's one thing to come to the theater every day and be abused," Casey said. "But it's a whole other thing when your best friend in the world is not only lying to you but hooking up with your abuser."

Oh, great. Some dirty little secret. Reese had opened her big mouth. "I never . . . lied to you," Brianna said.

Casey whirled around to face her directly. "Can I ask you a question and get a really truthful answer? Am I a really bad ASM?"

"You're the best, Case . . ."

"I know the *best* means a lot to you, Brianna. Me, too. I have been working my butt off to live up to that. But you've been with *him* all week long. First you were taking his side, then you were joking with him, then meeting with him and Mr. Little—doing things with *him*. Okay, things were changing. I get that. I got it a while ago. But the whole time, you never said a word to me about it. All month long it's like I haven't existed for Steve. I don't exist for the interns. And now I feel like I don't exist for *you*."

"Oh, Casey. I'm not choosing him over you. I just want everyone to get along —"

"You must want it really badly, to leave with him in the middle of the party and spend the night at the beach—" Casey suddenly turned away, her face reddening. "I have a lot to do. And you need to talk to Mr. Little."

Brianna blanched. Casey knew. She knew everything.

As she bustled away, Brianna stormed around the

theater and into the dressing room. Reese was sitting in her chair, feet up on her makeup table, eating from a gold box of Godiva chocolates. "The square ones with the squiggle on the top?" she called out, gesturing to the box. "They are to die for."

"I'm not hungry," Brianna snapped, yanking out a chair next to Reese and looking directly into her eyes.

Reese recoiled, pulling her legs down. "Brianna . . . ?"

"Why did you tell her?" Brianna demanded. "This was supposed to be our secret. You said so!"

"It is!" Reese looked shocked and hurt.

"Casey knows."

"I didn't tell any of the *interns*. Casey is one of us."

"A *secret is a secret, Reese*. You know how Casey feels about Steve! How long before they all find out? You know how fast stuff spreads in the theater!"

"And you've *never* talked about me and Shawn to anyone in the DC?" Reese asked.

Brianna fell silent. "Well, that's a little different. You're not exactly hiding it. You guys are always together . . ."

"And how long before everyone notices that you and Steve are always together?" Reese shrugged. "You know how fast stuff spreads in the theater."

The words stung. Brianna caught sight of a small note tucked into Reese's mirror—the card from the chocolate box, which said *Dear Teresita . . . Sweets for the sweet . . . Your Tony*.

Brianna left the dressing room, trying desperately to ungrit her teeth. Reese was trying to make it seem like the two situations were the same—Reese and Shawn, Brianna and Steve. But they weren't. Reese had no interest in keeping a secret. She *loved* the idea that people knew about her and Shawn.

As Brianna neared the office, she spotted Mr. Little emerging, his cell phone at his ear. "Ah, Brianna, my lifesaver—I was about to try you again. We've had a change of plans. Mr. Aldrich from the state arts council can only meet me at four o'clock. But alas, yet another awful crisis! My pals at Smitty's Auto Body Shop—in your beloved Ridgeport—have promised me my repaired Corvette today, which they've been holding hostage for two weeks. I need desperately to prepare for this meeting, so could you get a volunteer to accompany you to Smitty's? Perhaps Reginald?" Mr. Little waggled his eyebrows.

"His name is Steve," Brianna said.

"Ah, yes. You will, of course, drive at extremely slow speeds through backstreets," Mr. Little said, holding out his keys. "Won't you?"

"Of course," Brianna said. She took the keys and stepped outside, quickly calling Steve's number on her cell.

After a few rings he picked up. "I'm on my way," his voice said. "I overslept. Your fault. Can we do it again?"

"Don't come into the parking lot," Brianna said. "I'll meet you at the curb in front of the theater."

Steve sped along Sunrise Highway, his wipers creating a wide streak as they smeared the drizzle on the windshield. "I should replace those," he said.

"They know," Brianna blurted out. "About you and me. Reese told Casey, which means all the DC people know."

Steve shrugged. "That's only three, besides you and Reese."

"Charles is one of the three," Brianna said. "He can't keep a secret. Not to mention Reese . . ."

"That's trouble," Steve replied.

"I think Mr. Little knows, too. He suggested you go to the shop with me. And he did this thing with his eyebrows."

"He does that with everyone. The perv. Hey, look. We can't sweat it. It's summer stock. This kind of thing happens a lot. Everyone hooks up with everyone else, and then, boom, it's September and life starts again."

"Oh?" Brianna said. "Is that the game? We get to do this till September and that's it?"

"No! It's just . . . you know what I mean . . ." He suddenly took a left on Brookside Avenue.

"Where are you going?" Brianna asked. "Smitty's is on this street."

"I know. I want to see your school."

"Why?"

Steve shrugged. "Curious. It's good to know the enemy. Do you really have a Wall of Fame?"

"Yes, but—"

"With mummified Tony winners, and pictures of guys in drag and bear costumes?"

"No mummies. And they didn't call it drag a hundred years ago. It was when the place was a boys' school. *Steve, why do you want to do this?*"

"And if you stare long enough, you see yourself in the

photos, like magic? And that's like this rite of passage for students?"

"It's summer!"

"So, what school is closed in July? You guys don't have summer school? Sports practice? Team workouts?"

They pulled up in front of Ridgeport High. The front doors were swinging open and shut with student traffic. Just inside the front door, the janitor, Mr. Ippolito, was cleaning up a pile of wrappers and empty cups. Seeing them, he grabbed his broom handle like a microphone and began singing, "Briaaaanaaaaa!" to the tune of "Maria."

"This is Steve, Mr. Ippolito," Brianna said. "Mr. Ippolito was a star in many Ridgeport High productions."

"Five," Mr. Ippolito said. "I was on the, uh, five-year plan, if you catch my drift."

Brianna led Steve inside and showed him the wall, a collection of photos dating back to 1907 with a special display case devoted to the five RHS alums who had won Tony Awards—every inch of glass, every gilded frame polished to a sheen by Mr. Ippolito. "This is mad cool," Steve said, his face turned upward in wonder. Then his smile suddenly vanished. "Oh my God, *right there!*"

"Where?" Brianna said. "What?"

"Him!" Steve pointed to a guy playing the Pirate King in a 1956 production of *Pirates of Penzance*. "That's me!"

Brianna looked closely. The guy didn't look a thing like Steve—but that was to be expected. That was the legend. If you had theater in your blood, you saw yourself. Even if no one else did.

"Hoo boy . . ." Mr. Ippolito said. "He's bit."

As he whistled away, pushing his broom, Steve continued gaping at the display. "You guys are so lucky."

"Now you really hate us, huh?"

Steve shook his head. "Now I want my parents to move."

Eeeeeee . . .

Steve pulled Mr. Little's Corvette to a stop in the theater parking lot with a squeal of brakes. Following behind him, Brianna felt her heart racing. She hoped Mr. Little hadn't seen Steve's maneuver. "You nearly gave me a heart attack," she said, gliding to a stop beside him.

"I'm tempted to steal this baby," Steve said, admiring the dashboard.

Casey appeared in the front canopy of the theater. Her face was taut. "Where were you?"

"Picking up Mr. Little's car from the shop," Brianna said.

"No one told me," Casey said, staring incredulously at Steve. "I was looking all over for you. Mr. Bishop and Mr. Bunt just gave notes. We're putting in some changes."

"Damn," Steve said. "Well, you wrote them down, right?"

"Except for the ones I missed, trying to find you!" Casey said. "The point is, I need to be notified if you're leaving—"

"It was an emergency," Brianna said.

"—and most of all, Ms. Richards needs to be notified! I think you owe her an explanation."

"Okay," Steve said, tossing the car keys to Brianna. "I'll do that now."

As he walked away, Casey gave Brianna a bewildered, wounded look. "You could have asked me to come with you."

"Then *you* would have missed the notes," Brianna said.

"That's not the point," Casey replied.

"Case, you don't like driving anyway—"

"That's not the point either."

"Let's not argue," Brianna said. "Look, Mr. Little suggested Steve go with me, and it just didn't occur to me to ask you instead. I'm sorry."

Casey turned and stormed away. "Some of us have work to do," she said, letting the tent flap close behind her.

21

"THANK YOU, LADIES AND GENTLEMEN—SEE you at the next show and have a safe trip home!" blared Mr. Little's recorded voice over the speakers.

The last show of the week. Reese couldn't believe it. July 13 and halfway done.

Her face felt raw as she left the dressing room. As always, it had taken a long time and a lot of cold cream to get off all her makeup. Her face was going to be so happy when this show was over.

Heading across the walkway, she tried to ignore the screams coming from behind the fence:

"Hi! Do you know if Shawn is still here?"

"Were you in the show?"

"Can we get Shawn's autograph?"

"You were great!"

"Where's Shawn?"

Looking over her shoulder to make sure no cast or interns were watching, Reese darted into Shawn's dressing room and quietly closed the door. "Booty call."

"That's subtle," Shawn said with a wry smile, wiping makeup off his face.

Reese slapped him. "I mean, out there! They want you!"

"My public will have to wait," he said.

Reese pulled him aside and sat on his lap. "You sounded amazing today."

Shawn reached out and pulled her closer. "You know, I was watching you today, during the dance at the gym . . ."

"Don't say that," Reese moaned. "The dance was a piece of caca. The girls were phoning it in, Mr. Fredericks was half asleep, and José was late on his cue at the end."

"I didn't notice," Shawn said. "I was supposed to be looking at Maria, but all I could see was you."

"Is that a line?"

Shawn laughed, cocking his head curiously at her. "You don't even know it, do you? The effect you have on a stage?"

"No." Reese nestled closer. "Tell me more."

"Well, it's . . ." Shawn seemed to be searching for words. "Okay, you know that character in *Chorus Line*—Cassie? She doesn't fit into the line, because—"

"She's too good. Too unique. She steals focus. She's a star, and she can't help it."

"Exactly."

"That's me?"

Shawn nodded.

"That's the way I always wanted to be!" Reese said.

"Well, you're doing it. Totally."

"I can't believe you're telling me this!" Reese squealed, hugging him tightly. "I mean, people have said that to me. Mostly friends and family. But they just want to make me feel good. You're not just saying that to make me feel good?"

"I work with stars—everybody in my life is a star. I know what it takes. If you come to L.A., you'll see what I mean. A lot of kids can sing and dance, they're a dime a dozen. But they don't have that *thing* that makes you stand up and take notice."

"Ooh, I love when you say that." Reese grabbed both sides of his face and planted a kiss on his lips. "Okay, when?"

"When what?"

"When am I going out to L.A.?"

Shawn shrugged. "Anytime. The show is over in a week."

"You mean it? I can go back with you?"

"Well, I have a plane ticket, but the theater paid for it—"

"But if I got a ticket, too? You would help me? You'd introduce me to the right people?"

"If you're serious," Shawn said, "yeah, sure. My agent, Hilda, is a star maker. She did it for me. She would know exactly what to do with you."

"But where would I live?"

A smile passed across Shawn's face like a weather front. "Well, we could figure something out . . ."

Reese melted into him, parting her lips as he leaned back in his chair. Outside, fans were still yelling for Shawn, hoping he would appear, sign their programs or foreheads or arms and somehow magically anoint their lives. But this was real. This was true. Shawn Nolan had asked her to go back with him, and all Reese could think of was yes.

Yes. She would take the flight.

Yes. She would live in L.A. with the hottest star in Hollywood.

Yes. She would accept his help and work work work until her fame caught up with his.

Whap whap whap whap whap!

Reese jumped back at the noise from the door. Before she could climb off Shawn, it opened.

"We have to close up," Lauren said dully, standing with one hand on hip. "Mr. Little asked me to tell you . . ."

Reese stepped away from Shawn, smoothing out her clothes. "Oh. Um, okay."

"Sorry to interrupt," Lauren said with a big sigh. "Next time I'll turn my back. I didn't realize, but I guess I wasn't thinking . . ."

As she walked away, yawning, Shawn burst out laughing. "Right out of a script for *Posse Malibu.*"

Reese grinned, snuggling back into his lap. "Where were we?"

"I lost my place," Shawn whispered into her ear, which tickled her and made her laugh out loud.

"We"—she nibbled his ear—"were going to L.A.

together . . ." She kissed his neck. ". . . and I was going to become a star with Matilda's help . . ."

Shawn howled. "It's *Hilda*."

"Shut up," Reese said, pressing her lips against his and kissing him deeply.

As she staggered out of Shawn's dressing room, Reese had no idea what time it was. But she didn't care. She felt as if the ground were shifting beneath her.

"God, it's late," she said, finally checking her watch.

"It's seven-thirty in L.A.," Shawn replied, pulling his door shut as he stepped out behind her. "I'll give you a ride."

"I need to get my stuff," Reese said, heading for the girls' dressing room.

The grounds were silent—the theater, the various buildings, the walkway. She entered the darkened room and flicked on the light. Empty of people, it seemed so dead—so *small*—as if some magic image-enhancing spell had worn off. She saw the paint chipping off the cinder blocks in the corner, the cheapness of the folding chairs, the ratty gray pathway that had been trod into the maroon carpet behind the seats, the worn linoleum floor under that.

As she reached her spot, she saw her costume in a heap on the floor. The interns were supposed to have picked it up, but no one had been exactly in a hardworking mood tonight. She picked it up and hung it on an otherwise empty rack against the rear wall, hoping the wash would be done early tomorrow morning and that it hadn't already been done tonight. She sighed. If she had to put this sweaty thing on tomorrow, she would raise holy hell.

With a professional wardrobe staff, Reese thought, this kind of thing would never happen.

One more week. Then it would be good-bye to summer stock on Long Island.

In Hollywood, things would be way different.

22

"GOOOOD EVENING, CAMPERS—IT'S HALF HOUR!"
Ms. Richards chirped, poking her head into the dressing
room the next day.

Reese lifted the clothes that lay across Rosie's dressing-
room seat. Rosie was off vocalizing. All over the dressing
room, the other cast members were searching through
their stuff. "It's gone, Ms. Richards!" Reese said. "I put it
away last night myself. Everyone's been helping me look,
but it's gone."

"What is, sweetie?" Ms. Richards said.

"My *costume!*" Reese said, failing completely at
sounding cool.

Now Lauren was barging into the dressing room,
followed by Ariel Gruber, the costume head. "Where did
you put it?" Lauren demanded.

"*I put it away*," Reese said. "I came in here last night, in the dark, just after I saw you, to get ready to go. It's a good thing I did—because no one had picked up my costume from the floor. So I put it away myself." She gestured to the rack where she had hung her garments the night before. "And now it's gone."

"You hung it on *this* rack?" Ariel asked.

"Oy," Lauren groaned.

"Reese, that rack is for dry cleaning," Ms. Richards said wearily. "We generally don't use it until the end of the run, or in emergencies. Unless we tell them to rush it, the dry cleaner takes a couple of days. Your costume must have been sent out."

"So what am I supposed to wear?" Reese said. She looked at the clock. Twenty-eight minutes to curtain.

"We'll look for something in the shop," Ariel replied. "I'm sure we can figure this out."

As the two costume people left, Ms. Richards put her arm around Reese. "It'll work out."

"Thanks," Reese said, nodding. "I—I have to get something to drink . . ."

She ran out of the dressing room and knocked on Shawn's door. There was no answer. He was probably warming up in the Green Room.

Heading in that direction, she ran smack into Charles. "Darlin', I heard what happened. You have nothing to fear. Oscar de La Scopetta is here. Thirty minutes is plenty of time."

"Twenty-seven minutes."

"By the way, have you seen the monstrosity they are planning to give you?"

Before Reese could answer, Ariel emerged from the costume shop behind him with a pink frilly dress that looked like it came from a seven-year-old's birthday party. "This will have to do," she said.

Reese's jaw dropped. "I can't wear *that*," she said.

Charles politely took the costume for her. "Oh, yes, you can," he said.

"Charles, I won't be caught dead in that!" Reese said.

"Right this way," Charles said, heading toward the girls' dressing room. "At de La Scopetta's, all customers get free parking, free alterations. *Cover yourselves, girls!*"

Reese followed Charles as he whisked through the dressing room and out the back door. He went straight for the costume room, yanking open the door despite the sign that said DO NOT ENTER.

"There may be a certain *punge* of mildew in here," Charles said, grabbing a seam ripper off a shelf, "but we'll be quick. First we break down . . ." He began ripping the frills off the dress's shoulder. Then he tore off the pink sash and pulled down the hems. ". . . And then we build up."

Rummaging around the shelves, he yanked out a couple of shoe boxes and placed them on a table. "Ah, perfecto," he said, quickly but carefully removing a sexy red sash from one of them and a ruffle from another. Grabbing a needle and thread from the shelf, Charles furiously sewed the sash onto the waist of the dress, fixed the hems, and tacked the ruffle along the bottom. "And we *must* do something to satisfy the clamor for the world-famous Van

Clevage," he continued, snapping off two of the buttons and quickly sewing a new plunging neckline.

"Voilà," he said, holding out his creation and slowly turning it. "Does it meet with your approval?"

Reese smiled. He was a miracle worker. "My God, it's better than the old one!" she said, hugging him as she took the costume. "I love you."

Charles beamed. "All tips appreciated, we accept American Express."

"Turn around," Reese commanded, pulling down the strap on her tank top.

"Oh, yes, your famous modesty," Charles said as he looked toward the wall.

Reese quickly took off her street clothes and put on the dress, forcing it down over her hips.

The wall mirror didn't lie. She looked hot.

"It's tight," Charles said. She could see him appraising her in the mirror.

Reese grinned. "Were you watching me dress, Charles?"

"Darlin', if it gives you a little frisson, then yes. Now, I can let out the seam a bit so your boobies aren't so bulgy—"

"Don't you dare!" Reese looked at her watch. "We have only eight minutes."

She raced outside and around to the dressing room. Lauren and Ariel were still looking around one last time for Reese's original costume. Ms. Richards was on her cell phone. None of them looked particularly happy.

"Problem solved," Reese announced, striking a runway pose in her new costume.

Ariel's eyes went wide. "Where on earth did you find *that*?"

"Given to me by you, altered by Charles," Reese said, with a glance to the door, where Charles was giving a dramatic little bow.

"Well, well . . . mazel tov," Ms. Richards said.

Ariel nodded, impressed. "Not bad. You and I should talk sometime, Charlie . . ."

Lauren, kneeling under the rack in a pile of clothes, threw them into a box. Without saying a word, she stormed out.

Ms. Richards sighed, looking at her watch. "Okay, it's time for the five-minute call . . . can you . . . oh my God . . ."

She clutched her midsection, her face quickly losing color.

"Carol?" Ariel rushed toward her. "Are you all right?"

"Oh dear . . ." Ms. Richards said. "I think—I may be—"

A pained smile distorted her face. The rest of the cast were up out of their seats, gathering around.

Ariel took Ms. Richards's arm and began walking her outside. "*Someone call Dr. Lansdale, quick!*" she shouted over her shoulder. "*Ms. Richards is in labor!*"

23

"LADIES AND GENTLEMEN, THE SANDY SHORES
*Playhouse, fifty years of Broadway in the burbs, thanks you
for your patience in this brief but unavoidable delay. We
will be beginning momentarily . . ."*

Mr. Little's jolly voice echoed through the dome like
a cheerful airline pilot telling you not to worry that the
plane is bucking like an angry bull at thirty-five thousand
feet.

Casey frantically looked through her notes. Ms.
Richards's car was disappearing out of the parking lot. Her
husband, who'd just arrived at the theater, was behind
the wheel. Dr. Lansdale, the theater's official doctor, had
promised to contact Ms. Richards's obstetrician. From
her symptoms, she was very close.

Struggling to pay attention to the show, Casey circled all the cue changes in red, making sure to thoroughly cross out all the discarded ones. With Ms. Richards off having a baby, she and Steve would be calling cues and troubleshooting everything.

She was not looking forward to this.

They'd called a ten-minute delay, which was almost over. The audience was sounding restless. Casey checked her watch. Just about time for—

"Places for Act One!" Steve's voice resounded through the dressing-room speakers. He had gotten to the mike first.

She ducked into the theater through the six-o'clock aisle entrance, opposite the dressing rooms. Steve was in the corridor behind the seats, hanging up the mouthpiece on a hook in the wall. Next to him Mr. Little paced nervously, holding a cell phone to his ear.

"Thanks for doing that announcement, Steve," Casey said. "What's the news?"

Steve put an index finger to his lips. "Shhhh."

Mr. Little nodded, muttering something into the phone and flipping it shut. "Dr. Lansdale reports that she's in great shape. She's not in labor, just a few strong contractions. But the obstetrician has recommended bed rest for her until the big day." He placed one hand on each of their shoulders, flashing a warm smile. "Are you two ready? It'll be up to you to share the duties."

"I've got it under control," Steve shot back.

"Right," Casey said. "Me, too."

"I know you'll do fine," Mr. Little said, tapping them both on the shoulder and striding away.

The Jets had begun to assemble at the head of the ramp. "How is she?" Harrison asked.

"No baby yet, but she has to stay in bed." Casey looked at her watch and reached for a headset on a hook on the wall. But Steve got there first.

"House to half . . ." Steve said softly into the mouthpiece. "Orchestra . . . go!"

As the orchestra began playing, the Jets ran down from all the ramps, dancing as they hit the stage.

"Steve," Casey said, "about the cues—"

"I've got all the cues," Steve returned. "No problem."

"But there were some changes when—"

But Steve was already walking away, toward the four-o'clock exit, where Brianna had just entered.

Casey flipped her clipboard under her arm and walked out. Although Mr. Little had said that all the interns would be able to stay for the whole summer if they wanted—including Charles, Brianna, and Casey—she didn't want any part of it. Working with Steve had been a nightmare, and it needed to end.

Leaving the theater, she traveled around from door to door, asking if anyone needed help. She sewed a button on the costume of one of the Sharks. She burned some pieces of cork, which the guys used to smear fake bruises on their faces after the fight scene. She jumped in and out of the theater to watch certain scenes and check on Steve, who never seemed to need her help.

When she heard Shawn and Lacey starting to sing "One Hand, One Heart," she headed into the theater again. This was her favorite song in the show.

"Casey!" Callie's voice called from the scene shop. "Get over here!"

Casey turned. *Get over here?* Callie was picking up her technique from Steve. "Yes?"

"Come *on*, Scene Seven's about to end—we have to clear the bridal shop," Callie said, looking disheveled and frantic. "Amber just got sick on me and Marc smashed his finger with a hammer. Have you seen the set? *Three* mannequins and two of those old sewing machines—and all period authentic. The machines are the size of truck engines and the mannequins feel like they're made of lead. No way we can get them off in time. The last time we tried this it was a disaster. The Jets ran onstage for Scene Eight, singing about killing each other—with two dummies in bridal dresses behind them!"

"Yes, I remember." Casey checked her clipboard. "But I've talked to Mr. Fredericks about it. He's going to give you extra time. He'll vamp until you're done, and the boys won't come in until they hear those three chords that begin the Quintet."

"Fantastic. But he's going vamp the audience to sleep if I don't have more help—*now*!"

"One Hand, One Heart," which ended Scene Seven, was nearly over. Casey followed Callie into the theater, to the top of the ten-o'clock ramp, where three Sandy Shores interns, all looking a little undernourished, stood crouched and ready to run onto the stage. "I see what you mean," Casey whispered.

Steve was running toward them from six-o'clock, windmilling his arms and mouthing *"Go! Go!"*

Casey eyed the stage. Shawn was kissing Lacey's hand, the signal for the blackout. "Now," she said, running down the aisle as the spot faded to black.

As Shawn and Lacey scurried off the opposite side of the stage, Casey, Callie, and the interns took hold of the mannequins and sewing machines, pushing them toward ten-o'clock in near darkness. The orchestra was continuing to play "One Hand" softly under the set change. Casey worked fast, even though she knew Mr. Fredericks would vamp this music as long as necessary, until Ms. Richards cued him for—

Casey's heart skipped. Ms. Richards wasn't there. How would Mr. Fredericks know . . . ?

Suddenly the "One Hand" music stopped. The orchestra hit the opening chords of the next scene. Way too early.

Who was cuing this?

As she pushed the sewing machine, she spotted Steve at the top of the aisle, under a small reading light affixed to the wall. He was reading his clipboard. Casey realized he must have the *old* cue sheet without yesterday's updates.

He didn't know.

"*Move!*" Casey whispered, running.

She was not quite off the stage when the lights hit her full face. To a squall of trumpets, the Jets barreled onto the stage in full furious fight mode.

She felt like an idiot, stumbling down the stage ramp and finally up the aisle ramp toward the back of the theater.

"What was that all about?" Steve demanded as she reached the top of the ramp. Brianna was with him now, looking at Casey with bewilderment.

"We changed that cue, Steve!" Casey said. As she stepped outside, Brianna and Steve followed, with Callie close behind. "You were supposed to let Mr. Fredericks vamp the orchestra. You were supposed to keep your eye on the stage and wait."

"How was I supposed to know?" Steve said.

"*You should have been here when we made the change!*" Casey said. "Instead of driving around Ridgeport in a Corvette and ogling the Wall of Fame!"

"You could have told me," Steve said.

"You could have asked!" Casey shot back. "You could have asked for a copy of my cue sheet. But you don't *use* a cue sheet. You have it in your head—and when you forget, you check the only cue sheet you have, which is two weeks old!"

"Casey has a point," Brianna said.

"Maybe *she* should be calling the cues," Callie added.

Steve ripped the headset off his head. "She never asked."

"You didn't give me the chance!" said Casey. "You took the headset and—"

"*Yo! Psst! My ladder!*"

Shawn was peering out of the flap, his eyes wide.

Casey raced to his side and looked at the stage. The Jets and Sharks were singing furiously, and Anita was about to make her entrance. In moments, Shawn was supposed to enter, climbing his ladder and wailing out the song "Tonight" over all the rest of the singing.

But there was no ladder.

"My fault!" came Callie's voice. *"Here!"*

She had raced back to the shop and fetched a small stepladder, which Shawn grabbed, nearly beaning a tall man in the last row before racing down the ramp and onto the stage. Mercifully Mr. Fibich did not shine the spot on Shawn until *after* he had set his ladder down.

He made the entrance into the song perfectly.

"Whew," Casey said.

"I'm sooo sorry," Callie said.

Casey forced a smile. "We'll get it right next time."

"Nice job, kiddandos! Hot hot hot!"

Casey heard Mr. Bishop's voice from inside the theater, along with the rumble of footsteps to the dressing rooms. Finally the show had ended. As she hung up her headset, she spotted Steve walking toward her, an intent look on his face.

What now? she wondered. What had she done wrong?

Mr. Bishop peeked in from the flap, to her left. "May I talk to you for a moment?"

Casey swallowed hard. She followed him outside, happy not to have to face Steve but still trying to squelch the flutter in her stomach. She attempted to say "Yes?" but her throat was so dry it came out something like "Yuck?"

He smiled. "It was a good show, Casey, it really was, especially under the circumstances, with you kids taking over for Carol. Many, many kudos. But I have to ask you—what the heck happened with the transition to the Quintet?"

"Well, I wasn't fast enough—"

Steve's voice interrupted her from behind. "It was my fault."

Mr. Bishop looked past Casey. "Oh?"

"Casey has been on top of all the changes," Steve went on. "She's the one who should be calling the cues. She knows just as much as Ms. Richards. The problem was me. I grabbed the headset, and I didn't have the correct updates."

Casey couldn't believe her ears. Steve was looking at the floor, sheepishly, and he raised his eyes to Casey. "Sorry."

Mr. Bishop pinned Steve with his eyes. Now Casey was sure he was going to fire *him*.

Finally Mr. Bishop shrugged. A smile played at the edge of his face. "Seeing Tony run down that aisle, holding that stupid ladder . . . oh . . . oh my dear . . ."

He looked at Steve. Steve looked at Casey.

All three burst out laughing.

"Oh my," Mr. Bishop said. "I will compose myself and see you two tomorrow."

As he staggered away, his shoulders shaking, Casey and Steve walked back toward the Green Room. "Thanks," Casey said. "For being honest."

Steve shrugged. "Thank *you*. Brianna is totally right, you know. She says you're a genius."

"I'm not," Casey replied.

"Well, I'm really glad you're here. You're doing a good job."

"You are? I am?"

As Steve veered away toward Mr. Little's office, he gave her a friendly salute. Casey was too stunned to return it, so her hand raised uncertainly about halfway, as if she were patting an invisible giant dog.

As she headed toward the Green Room, Callie greeted her in the doorway, hands clasped stiffly behind her. "I need to talk to you."

"Look, I didn't do it," Casey said. "It was a misunderstanding—"

"No, it wasn't," Callie said with a disbelieving shake of the head.

Fwoosh. Casey felt the air rushing out of her. She didn't have the energy for this. Convincing them one by one was just too hard. "Callie, I'm trying my best—"

"So I hear," Callie said, slowly bringing her hands out from behind her. She was holding a faded bouquet of dusty plastic flowers. "From *Arsenic and Old Lace*, 1982. It's all I could find."

What? Casey looked at the flowers and then at Callie. "Is this some kind of joke?"

"I talked to Steve. I know what happened." Callie shrugged. "Peace?"

Casey was speechless. Numbly, she took the ugly flowers.

"He told all of us," Callie continued. "He told us a lot of things—during intermission, during the second act. And we all decided we weren't even angry at you guys.

It's like this attitude we started with—and we're hanging on to it, for no good reason. We've been really bad to you. But most of all me. So I want to apologize."

"Darling, those are *so* you!" Charles said, strolling toward the Green Room with Harrison, who had already changed out of his costume, and Reese, who was jeté-ing across the blacktop.

Casey took the flowers. She felt a tear trickle down her cheek. "You were just taking care of business . . ."

Callie shook her head. Her face was turning red. "No. Really." She heaved a sigh. "Remember . . . at the beach house . . . the food in your cars?"

"That was *you*?" Casey said.

"Lauren, too. But I was the ringleader. We were . . . I don't know . . . angry . . ."

Charles nodded. "I should have known. Vegans."

"Look, we all have so much in common," Callie said, looking around to Charles, Harrison, and Reese. "Let's put all the bad stuff in the past. I want to make it up to you—all of you. At the end of August, my parents are having a big birthday party for me on Fire Island—"

Reese froze. *"Oh my God—end of August?"*

"I hope you can all make it," Callie went on.

"Those photos!" Reese blurted out. "Of the beach party. On Nolanfan. *You* took them!"

"Uh . . . yeah . . ." Callie said curiously. "How did you know?"

Charles clapped his hands together. "Cuspbaby!"

"Aha!" Reese said.

"Doll, you are a genius!" Charles high-fived Reese as Callie looked bewildered.

A group of interns had gathered just behind her. One of them, a burly guy with a crew cut named Trevor, called out, "Hey, the usher guy! I saw them today for the first time."

Charles looked at him dubiously. "*And* . . . did you like them?"

"The best part of the show!" Trevor said with a grin. "Almost peed my pants."

"Well, thanks," Charles said brightly. "Next time, let me know. We have a stash of Depends in the ushers' lounge."

Marc, holding a plastic cup that had become unglued from a tray, barged by. "Personally, no offense, but about those ushers? I believe in honesty, okay, and I thought they were embarrassing."

"Marc . . ." Callie said plaintively.

Casey closed her eyes. It took one to spoil everything.

"Hate to spoil the lovefest," Marc replied with a shrug, heading for the prop room. "But they truly sucked."

Harrison rolled his eyes. "*Vre, 'sta diávola* . . ." he muttered.

Marc spun around. "Who are *you* to tell me to go to hell?"

"You . . . *understood* that?" Harrison said, looking stunned.

"*Ne, katalavéno—eimai Élinos,*" Marc said.

"Translation?" Reese asked.

"Yes, he understands, he's a Greek!" Harrison held out his arms to Marc. "*Patrióti!*"

"*Fíli mou!*" Marc replied.

They fell into each other, hugging and patting each other's back. In a manly way.

"I guess he won't be bothering you anymore," Casey said.

"Lucky me," Charles replied.

Lauren suddenly appeared in the door. She did a double take at Harrison and Marc. "Um, Marc, Callie, Trevor—I was going to tell you guys the time of the intern party—after the last show on Sunday?"

"I'll go," Marc said, putting one arm around Harrison and the other around Charles, "if they go!"

"And Casey and Brianna and Reese," Harrison added.

"*Ne!*" Marc declared. "Which, uh, sounds like *no* but means *yes.*"

"We are the Knights Who Say *Ne!*" Harrison blurted out.

Lauren paused a moment. "*Spamalot!*"

"Oh dear God," Charles muttered, "they play those games, too . . ."

Lauren looked at Casey. Casey shrugged.

"I guess . . . yeah, you guys are invited, too," Lauren said.

"Accepted!" Charles blurted out.

"Definitely!" Casey added.

"*Ne!*" said Harrison and Marc at the same time.

Marc gave Charles's shoulder an affectionate squeeze.

"God bless America and don't forget the Greeks," Charles said with a shrug.

Part 3
Tonight

July 20

24

IMPOSSIBLE.

Reese stood at the top of the ramp, watching the Jets and Sharks carry Shawn to the ground after his death scene, same as every night.

Same as every night, Shawn murmured "Ouuuuch," like E.T., just as he got out of earshot of the last row of the audience.

After letting him down, the Sharks raced to the other side of the stage to be in position for curtain call.

When all was in place, on a cue from Casey, Reese sprinted with the girls onto the stage for the Sharks-Jets curtain call. As she curtsied, she winked sexily to the nerdiest guy she could find in the audience.

Same as every night.

It was almost autopilot by now. They had been doing this for two weeks, and it seemed as if they would continue doing it, living through this drama, these songs, these tragedies, forever and ever and unto the ages, amen.

The crowd rose to its feet even before Shawn came onstage, same as every night. And when he did, taking his time, letting the light catch every glisten of sweat on his face, raising his arms outward in a gesture of embrace, they exploded—screaming, stomping, wanting him.

Impossible, Reese thought. It was all over. They would never do this again. It was as if they had built a living thing—a world from the printed page—and then tossed it aside. The set would be struck, the magic show would begin on Tuesday. The ensemble would start rehearsing *Guys and Dolls* that same day, to be performed after the magic show closed, and the cycle would build again.

She heard José's voice call "Go!"—the chorus's cue to exit and let Shawn have the stage to himself for a final solo "star" bow. Reese caught Shawn's eye and blew him a quick kiss. He grinned.

As she ran back up the ramp for the last time, she had a funny feeling she had never experienced before. Was there a word for the reverse of nostalgia? Not dwelling on the glories of the past, but the future? That's what she was feeling—a sadness overpowered by a to-her-toes excitement about tomorrow, and next week, and the rest of the summer.

Brianna, Casey, and Charles were waiting for her at the back of the house. "You were *soooooo* good!" Brianna screamed, hugging Reese and lifting her off her feet.

"Wonderful, Reese," Casey said. "I'm so proud of you."

"Doll, if you were any sexier, at least three of my Charlushers would have had a stroke," Charles said.

Mr. Little appeared, brandishing a cell phone. "I have a message for you all," he said. "But we have to come outside."

The entire cast followed him out the exit, to the area in front of Mr. Little's office. Inside the theater, Shawn was giving a little speech to the audience, thanking them and answering questions.

"Gather around—we can tell Shawn about this later," Mr. Little said, fussing with the phone. "How do I put this on speakerphone, Evangeline—I mean, *Brianna*?"

Brianna gently reached over and pressed a button on Mr. Little's cell.

"I hear there's good news tonight," came Ms. Richards's voice through the speaker, sounding a little craggy. "Two solid sellout weeks and the best performance of *West Side Story* ever!"

"YEAHH!" the cast shouted in return, but Mr. Little quickly shushed them. "And *your* good news, Carol dear?"

Her voice was soft and crackly, barely audible. "Philip . . . Edward . . . Richards," she said. "Say something, sweetie . . ."

Over the tinny speaker came a series of quick agitated squeaks, like a lost hamster.

"IT'S A BOY!" José shouted.

Everyone blurted out at once, cheering and screaming

and whistling and shouting congratulations—so much so that they could hear the audience inside the theater react with a baffled laugh.

One by one, the cast took turns congratulating Ms. Richards over the phone. After Reese's turn, she linked arms with Charles. "That baby will have so many aunts and uncles next summer," she said.

"Poor kid," Charles replied.

As they walked slowly to the dressing room, Brianna, Harrison, and Casey quietly linked arms with them, forming a chain.

Harrison swung them around on a detour, to the field in back of the theater. They stood at the edge, looking up silently. The sky was clear, the Milky Way arching overhead like a swoosh of white paint flung skyward. Reese wanted to reach up and grab the stars, to pull her face into them. She would tell them everything, but right now she wanted to taste the moment.

Harrison sighed. "God, I loved doing this show."

"Two weeks goes by so fast," Charles said.

"*Guys and Dolls* will be fun," Casey added without conviction.

"Yeah, for you interns . . . sniff, sniff," said Harrison. "We actors are out of a job."

"Mr. Little hinted there might be some spots in *Pajama Game*, later in the season," Brianna said. "Maybe he'll let us audition. Reese, there's a great dancing role in that."

Reese took a deep breath. Might as well just come out with it. "I would audition for it," she said. "If I were here. If I weren't going to L.A."

"Going *where?*" Harrison asked.

"To Hollywood," Reese said, grinning, "with Shawn."

They were all staring at her now. They were in shock. Of course. But they would understand. If anyone would get it, the DC would.

"Reese, it's been a big day . . ." Brianna said.

"I know—it sounds unbelievable," Reese replied, the words spilling out. "But Shawn's been amazing to me. He *so* believes in my talent. Of course he knows it will take time—maybe a couple of months or even till the end of the summer—but he's convinced I'll make it. He's going to introduce me to *his agent*—can you believe it? And they're casting two new shows on the CW, which he says I am *perfect* for—that's his word, *perfect*."

"Do your mom and dad know about this?" Harrison asked.

"I told them I'm going to stay with my cousin Ellen, who's at UCLA in the drama program. Which I'm not, of course. But she's in on this—"

"Whoa, whoa, slow down, sugar, before we all have heart attacks," Charles said. "You are *not* serious, right? Go ahead, tell me—'Charlesie-poo, I am pulling your big, stupid, gullible leg.'"

"I'm serious, Charles," Reese said resolutely. "I am going to do it. I'm going to be what you always said I should be."

"A Laker Girl?"

Reese kicked him. "A star!"

"Reese, um . . ." Harrison leaned against the wood-post fence. "I can see you doing this—I mean, I always thought you would, after college, maybe after grad school—but *now*? You're sixteen!"

"But I look eighteen," Reese said.

"And you're going to live with this guy?" Brianna said. "Have you really thought through the consequences of this?"

"You don't even have a diploma," Harrison said.

"Thank you, Mommy and Daddy," Reese replied.

"It'll be hard to just arrive there and step into auditions," Casey said. "Do you even have a head shot?"

"I'll get one when I'm there," Reese said.

"Head shots are expensive," Charles said.

"Shawn has more money than he knows what to do with," Reese said. *"Why are you asking me all these questions?"*

They all exchanged nervous glances. "Because we care about you," Casey finally said.

"Oh?" Reese couldn't stand this. Face-to-face—Charles, Brianna, Harrison, even Casey—*none* of them looked happy or excited. "Then why do I feel so beaten up right now? I thought you were my best friends. You're jealous, aren't you? You can't even see past your own egos and be happy for me!"

"Sweet cheeks, that's not it at all," Charles said softly.

From inside the theater, where Shawn was still talking to the closing-night audience, came a wave of laughter.

"That's what I want," Reese said. "What *he* has. I can always get a high school diploma and a college degree. But I will *pay* for that college degree myself, and every school will want me—because that's what happens to

stars. Colleges fight for them. You guys can do whatever you want with your lives, but I'm not stupid enough to pass up an opportunity like this."

That was all she had patience for. They would not wreck her last night in New York. She turned and walked away, back to the theater.

She would listen to Shawn, the one person who really understood her.

25

"WHO'S GOT A MATCH?"

Reese was vaguely aware of the interns shouting.
Something about a bonfire lit. Old newspapers.

They hadn't expected Shawn at the beach party. But
they had invited Reese, and Shawn came with her. Now
they were all running around trying to impress.

But Reese wasn't paying much attention. Her eyes were
closed. She could hear the bonfire crackle to life as she
pulled away reluctantly from a long kiss. "Wow. You are
really, really good at that."

"I can do better," Shawn said.

She felt his mouth envelop hers again, warming her
against the chill of the early-summer night. She loved
the taste of it but also the sound of their lips, parting

and meeting, like raindrops against a windowsill. As they sighed and lay on their sides, their bodies nestled into the sand, Reese traced every contour of his face.

She hadn't told him yet. She figured she would just surprise him at the airport. She had managed to book a seat on the same flight. She would be in economy and he'd be in first class, but who cared? Working it out with her parents was easier than she expected. Her cousin in L.A. had agreed to lie on her behalf—the word was that Reese would be staying with her in UCLA for a few weeks.

In the flickering light of the fire, Reese surveyed the party. A few of the interns were lugging a big pot of clams, mussels, and crab claws to the fire. Amber and Ariel had a crate full of lobsters, and Amber was moaning about how she didn't want to see them die. Marc and Lauren were locked in an embrace. Harrison, talking as usual, had his arms around Callie—which was a new development. From a couple of blankets away, Brianna and Steve were laughing at some private joke. And Charles was ringing the whole site with tiki torches.

Reese smiled. God, she was going to miss them all. "What's it like?" she asked Shawn. "Life in Hollywood . . ."

"You'll find out," Shawn replied with a tiny smile. "You drive a lot. Parties. Lots of beach. Surfing. And when you're shooting, you spend a lot of time waiting around, in between bursts of really, really hard work. Sometimes boring, most of the time fun. It's worth it."

"Sounds amazing."

Shawn angled his watch so he could see the face of it in

the reflected light. "Listen," he said softly, sitting up. "I'm sorry, but I have to get my beauty sleep . . ."

"Yeah, right," Reese said, pulling him down to the blanket.

"I know, I'm a wuss," Shawn said with a grin. He unclasped her fingers and stood up. "Seriously, Reese, I have to wake up mad early. I'm being driven to Manhattan for a *breakfast* meeting with my agents, then I'm supposed to do some PR stuff before catching a two o'clock flight. But don't worry, there's more where this comes from."

"So . . . you're going back to the house alone?" Reese said.

He knelt, leaning down to kiss her. "You know where to find me on the West Coast."

"And I will," she said, throwing her arms around him.

Their last kiss was long and deep, as lasting as a memory and as solid as a promise. "I can't wait," he said.

Standing up, Shawn called out, "You guys? You were the best crew I ever worked with! I hope to see you all again next year! And if any of you ever end up in L.A., I will take it personally if you don't look me up, okay?"

Everyone rose, and Shawn began circulating through the interns, embracing each one and saying good-bye. Brianna and Steve groggily sat up to take their turn, along with Callie and Harrison, and Casey and Charles.

That was sudden.

Reese fought off the feeling. He wasn't rejecting her. He was a star. Stars had lives that were different. They had to be selfish, a little. They had to look good in the morning.

Reese realized she might as well go home, too. Take his example. There was a lot to do before tomorrow's flight. As she began gathering up her stuff, Charles quickly sidled up to her. "Don't do anything I wouldn't do."

"For your information, Shawn and I are going our separate ways tonight," Reese said.

"What? My imagination was already running wild," Charles said.

Reese felt her eyes welling up. What was she going to do without Charles? "Oh God, I'll miss you," she said, throwing her arms around him.

"Uh, Reese," Harrison said, "you'll see him on Tuesday."

Reese shook her head and started for her car. "I have to pack."

"Pack?" Casey piped up. "For what?"

"For L.A.," Reese said. "I told you I was going. Shawn is having lunch with his New York agents, and I'm meeting him at the airport for a two o'clock flight."

"*Tomorrow?*" Charles said.

Brianna, who was nibbling on Steve's ear, spun so fast she nearly took out a chunk. "Reese, you are out of your goddamn mind."

"Reese, just hold on a minute," Harrison called out.

They were all following her to her car. *Yelling* at her.

She knew she shouldn't have said anything. Her gut had told her to keep quiet to her friends. Not to call them until she was at the airport. Waiting to board her flight.

"Reese, what *exactly* did Shawn say?" Brianna pestered. "Was it a definite invitation—or just like, 'You should come out to L.A.'?"

Opening the back door of her car and throwing in her stuff, Reese tried to keep her cool. "Guys," she said, "I already have the reservation. I feel bad about leaving. I feel terrible about missing you already. Why aren't you happy for me? You're acting like I'm going off to war!"

"Perhaps we are rushing into things a bit?" Charles said. "I mean, we don't want our little dancerslut running off with the first megahunk superstar she meets—"

Reese looked him in the eye. "Don't underestimate your little dancerslut, Charles. You all think you know me, but you don't. Shawn is the only one who sees. The only one who doesn't underestimate me. And I'm glad *someone* in my life is seeing me for who I am—and what I want."

"Reese, that's unfair . . ." Brianna said helplessly.

"This is a once-in-a-lifetime chance to get an agent and be seen," Reese said, "and you are *not* talking me out of it."

"There are tons of great agents in New York," Harrison said. "You don't have to go all the way to California to kick off your career."

"And for a dancer, hon, the Big Apple's the place to be," Charles said. "How many sitcoms are about dancing?"

"Shawn says there's lots of theater in L.A.," Reese said. "That's one of the things that makes me unique. He says I can do plays while I audition for roles in TV and film."

"I don't know how to say this," Harrison said, "but Shawn is a guy. A good guy, unbelievably talented and nice—but a guy. Guys make promises. What's in this for *him*, Reese?"

"Oh God, Harrison, you are a piece of work. If you're jealous about us hooking up, well, you had your chance . . ." She felt tears welling up as she opened the driver's door. "Why are you all attacking me? Don't any of you *get* this?"

"I get it, Reese," Casey finally spoke up. "I know what it's like to want to get away, start a new life."

A tear trickled down Reese's cheek, and she quickly wiped it away. "Thank you," she said.

"But you're going to miss us," Casey continued, "more than you know. And we won't be the same."

Brianna nodded. "We need you in Drama Club, Reese. It's senior year. Please—at least *think* about what this will do to us. Think about what a great year you'll have—*we'll* have—if you stay."

Reese took a deep breath. She couldn't look in Casey's or Brianna's eyes. Honestly, she hadn't really thought that part through. Imagining the year at Ridgeport—new shows, lead roles—it would be awesome.

But this was about reality. About seizing her chance for a career while it was still hot. "I—I just need to see what happens, guys. And where things are going with Shawn. If things don't work out, I can always come home."

She gave one last look at them. Managing a smile, she opened the car door, climbed in, and turned the key.

She pulled out of the lot without looking back.

26

CHARLES HAD NOT SLEPT ALL NIGHT. HE HATED not sleeping. He especially hated not sleeping and then taking the two-hour drive to Kennedy Airport, where there were too many reflective surfaces to avoid looking at your sad self every few seconds.

"Are you sure it was *Kennedy* Airport?" he asked, looking nervously at the time on the departures screen— 12:34. "What if she's at La Guardia or Newark? Or Islip MacArthur, God forbid?"

"I saw the e-ticket on her dashboard," Casey said. "Flight two-seventeen, Kennedy Airport, leaving for Los Angeles at two-oh-three—and it matches the flight right there on the screen. We have plenty of time. But the important thing is to move fast when she shows up. I'll play lookout by the entrance."

Charles watched her go and started pacing, looking out to the curb every time a vehicle pulled up. Harrison and Brianna were sitting, eating McMuffins and staring bleakly out the window.

"Now! *Now!*" Casey came running toward them from the sliding doors. "She's getting out of a taxi!"

"She hasn't lost her sense of style," Charles said, reaching into a large canvas bag and pulling out a roll of stylish fabric, affixed with large images of Reese looking fabulous (not hard to find) and Reese Photoshopped into archival pictures of Ridgeport plays from the Wall of Fame (much too much hard work until the wee hours of the morning).

Brianna was holding a banner that said RIDGEPORT LOVES REESE!

Harrison had a huge blowup of Reese in *Godspell*, grinning confidently at the audience—over the words DON'T LEAVE, VAN CLEVE!

Casey had a simple placard on a stick, which she held high: THE DC NEEDS YOU, REESE!

Reese wearily rolled her suitcase into the terminal. She yawned as she glanced around at the airline counter. She nearly collided with Harrison. And then her jaw dropped.

"Oh. My. God."

"*And-a one . . .*" Harrison muttered—the signal for him and Charles to start singing "You Gotta Have Reese" to the tune of "You Gotta Have Heart" from *Damn Yankees*—which fell apart dismally after about eight bars.

Which meant an early cue for their unison cheer:

"*Gimme an* R, *gimme an* E, *gimme an* E-S-E! *Come on home to the old DC!*"

"Quiet!" came a tired voice from an elderly person in the check-in line.

"New Yorkers," Charles muttered.

Reese's shoulders slumped. "I don't believe this . . ."

Charles couldn't tell what she was feeling behind those dark specs. The slumpage could mean an utter change of heart and a willingness to forswear her foolish ways, or, more likely, *I am SO sick of you by now and would very much like to blink three times and see you gone.*

"We love you," Casey said hopefully, putting her placard down and holding her arms out to Reese. As she moved closer, wrapping her arms around her friend, Reese stood stock still.

Charles quickly draped his fabric around himself, striking a fetching pose. "If you stay, you can wear this."

Finally. A lip twist in a vaguely upward direction, resembling in shape, if not in spirit, a smile.

"Thoughts?" Charles said. Weight shift, new pose.

"I look good on you," Reese said in a barely audible voice.

A flash went off as a smiling tourist snapped a picture.

"The paparazzi, *again*," Charles huffed. "Talk to my agent, please!"

"I—I don't believe you all came out here—all the way for me," Reese said.

"You're one of the family," Casey said.

"We won't be the DC without you," Brianna added.

Reese took a deep breath. She took off her glasses,

wiping her eyes with her sleeve. "You really feel that way? Even you, Harrison?"

"Of course," Harrison replied.

"Have you ever doubted it?" Casey asked.

"Me? Slutty, aggressive, over-the-top, obnoxious me?" Reese smiled. "I've always been the weird one."

Brianna offered her a tissue. "Yeah, you are all those things."

"Totally," Charles said.

"But which one of us isn't over-the-top?" Brianna continued. "Charles with designing, Casey with schedules, Harrison with acting, me with . . . well, everything. That's why we stick together, Reese. Look at this summer. *This* is where you belong, Reese, not in some strange place. Please stay with us."

"I—I love you guys, too," Reese said quietly. "But . . . things change. Dreams . . . don't have, like, schedules. I'm sorry." She grabbed the handle of her suitcase. "I have to check in . . ."

Paralyzed, Charles watched her turn away. It hadn't worked. Never in a million years did he think she would be following through with this, really leaving. Reese needed attention and love. They had given it to her, poured it out . . .

"Reese . . ." Brianna said.

"Leave her," Harrison whispered.

Charles fought back a tear. Harrison was right. They couldn't stop her. And that meant he'd be without his best friend in the DC.

Suddenly Reese stopped. She glanced at her watch,

then looked at the door. "Did you guys see Shawn?" she asked over her shoulder.

"Nope," Casey replied.

"That's funny," Reese said. "I—I was going to surprise him, but I broke down and called him last night—woke him up. He said he would be here—at the check-in counter—around noon at the latest. His agent was meeting him for breakfast and paying for a limo to take him here."

"Maybe he's at the gate already," Charles muttered.

Reese pulled her cell phone from her pocket and tapped out his number. "Voice mail . . . Hey, big guy. It's me. I'm at the airport check-in. Where are you? Call. Can't wait!"

As she hung up, Charles noticed a small, wiry guy in blue polyester khakis and a white monogrammed shirt snooping around the placards and banners. "Helloooo?" Charles sang. "Those are ours . . ."

The guy stood up, eyebrows furrowed, and glanced at a thick manila envelope in his hand. Charles could see the monogram now—*Frank/Swift-E Messenger Service*. "One of you Reese Van Cleve?" he asked.

"Yeah . . ." Reese said dubiously.

"Please sign," said Frank, shoving the package and a sheet of paper toward her. "Quickly, please, ma'am, I'm illegally parked."

All of them gathered around the thick envelope. The return address read Maurice Bender & Associates, LLC.

Nervously Reese signed and returned the sheet. As Frank darted away like a track star, she ripped opened the envelope and pulled out the contents.

Unfolding in her hand was a yellow-orange T-shirt with a colorful logo:

POSSE MALIBU
SEASON THREE

Reese looked completely bewildered. "Shawn's show . . ."

An envelope, which had been tucked into the shirt, floated to the ground, and Charles quickly retrieved it.

Reese handed him the shirt and opened the note. As she read it, her face blanched.

"What is it?" Casey said.

"Read it, girl," Charles urged her.

But Reese just shook her head and held out the note:

Hey, Reese!

Sorry, but u'll never beleive this—I'm in the air already! So I can't contact u (of course). Wow. What a breakfast!!! Maury suprised me (the tool!! I hate suprises). But this is a good one he got me a PILOT for a new mystery thriller on Fox. Okay Orlando was supposed to play the roll but he couldn't do it at the last minute so I wasn't the first choice but STILL. A Great Part & they're trying to get Kiefer for my dad, which I will find out when I get there. It's in London and I luv that place so cheerio! Anyway, I will miss u & wl always think about this summer (mmmm). & don't forget, u should really look me up when ur in L.A. & I mean it.

Wish me luck,

SN

27

REESE HELD HER STOMACH AND REFUSED TO SIT. They were telling her to sit but her feet were moving, moving fast and toward the ladies' room. She was aware of their voices, of Charles asking the rest of them to let her go, saying she was sick—but she wasn't sick. Not sick at all.

She wasn't anything. Not well, not angry, not happy, not human. She was a net, a framework that you could see through, poke fingers through—airy and absent— something put together with strings of flesh.

The bathroom was bright and empty. Someone was in a stall, whispering to a child, telling the child to be patient, loving the child, and Reese locked herself in the next stall and listened to the soothing sound through the pounding of her own head.

"Reese?"

It was Casey. Reese could see Casey's red Converse sneakers peeking below the stall door. Funny how you could tell a person's mood from the angle of their feet. She was asking if Reese was okay, and Reese wanted to laugh, to ask Casey how you defined *okay* when someone had just reached inside and yanked out your guts. When a big, beautiful life you were about to jump into turned into a black gaping hole.

The door was swinging open now and Reese reached out quickly in order to—what? Shut it in Casey's face?—but her fingers jammed against the metal and she just stood there, arm half raised, legs bent because of the cramped toilet, when Casey took her hand and pulled her out. "Hey, it's going to be all right," she said.

"It's going to be all right," said the image of Casey in the mirror over the sink.

"It's going to be all right," said the mom in the stall to her kid, and Reese would have burst out laughing if she hadn't seen her own face in the mirror, which was decidedly not all right.

"He—" Reese said, feeling the blood rise to her head. "He—"

"He's a jackass," Casey declared.

And with those words, with that conviction, coming from Casey's mouth, Reese nestled her head into her friend's shoulder, crying and walking, walking and crying until they reached the terminal where the others were waiting.

They swarmed around her. "Let it out," Brianna said.

"We're here for you," Harrison added.

"Feel the love," Charles chimed in.

She wanted to laugh, this big scene in the middle of the airport, but she didn't. She let them surround her, hug her, rock with her, until Shawn went through the greatest tragic performance in his life, totally in her head, as multiple villains—with his face boiling in oil, falling from a cliff to be impaled by ragged spikes, being called before the firing squad, dying and living only to be dying again—until the images slowly settled and Reese once again heard the footsteps and clicks and distant dull voices of the check-in area.

"Flight two-seventeen, nonstop to Los Angeles, now boarding gate three," a voice echoed through the terminal.

"Well, I guess . . ." Brianna said uncertainly.

Reese reached into her pocket. The e-ticket felt so flimsy and insubstantial. She pulled it out, ripped it in half, then half again and again until it rained to the floor like confetti.

"Happy New Year," said Charles as he began scooping up the pieces.

"You can probably get a refund," Harrison said, "or credit for another flight."

"That's what I like about you, Harrison," Reese said weakly. "Straight from the heart."

Casey, Brianna, and Charles burst out laughing.

"She's ba-ack . . ." Charles said.

"It's true!" Harrison protested. "I mean, love is action, not just words."

Reese sank into a hard plastic seat. "I love you guys."

"So," Casey said, "what do we do now?"

"Something outrageous," Brianna said.

"I know!" said Charles in a way-too-chipper voice. "We could put on a show."

Brianna put a hand on his shoulder. "Not a bad idea. We can do that!"

"Where?" Harrison asked, glancing at the long lines that wound toward the ticket counters. "I'm not sure security would appreciate it right here."

"No," Brianna said, "but we do have a theater . . ." She pulled out her key chain and held it up, smiling slyly. "Mr. Little gave me the key so I could open for him when he has breakfast meetings. And I was thinking . . . the theater is dark Monday night. The magic show basically has no set, so we could conceivably use the stage for a karaoke night—for us and the Sandy Shores interns. Show tunes only!"

"Yes!" Reese said.

"Excellent idea!" Harrison agreed.

"I've been working on my Judy Garland," Charles said. "The late years."

"But will Mr. Little be okay with that?" Casey asked.

"I'll ask him. And Mom." Brianna smiled. "Sometimes it's good to pull rank."

"And now . . . ladies and gentlemen, direct from the Lower East Side of Manhattan . . ." Harrison's voice boomed out over the Sandy Shores Playhouse sound system. "Barbra Streisand!"

Reese nearly spat out her popcorn. Charles had found a shiny, straight-haired wig in the costume shop. Thankfully he had not tried to squeeze his plus-size frame into a gown, but the authentic-looking putty nose explained why he had taken so long to get ready. As he tore into "Don't Rain on My Parade," complete with slinky choreography, half the interns were looking clueless, asking for an explanation, while the other half were practically on the floor.

Steve and Brianna, who had sung a duet from *Spring Awakening* that was so hot Reese was still hyperventilating, were both collapsing over each other in hysterics.

Casey was nearly in tears of joy—and not completely due to Charles. Sitting next to her and holding tight to her hand was Chip, who had taken the train up from Johns Hopkins for the night, just for this.

The loudest, most helpless laughter of all came from Marc, who was trying to form a wolf whistle but was unable to shape his lips.

It was fitting for Charles to go last. The party had been a huge hit. By now nearly everyone had sung, including some unbelievably talented Sandy Shores interns. All the DC members had contributed—except Casey, who didn't like singing; and Kyle, who had been complaining of a stomach virus.

As Charles vamped across the stage, throwing back his head for the final verse, a bellow came from the back of the house that nearly drowned out the speaker system. "GOD BLESS AMERICA AND DON'T FORGET BAR-BA-RA STREISAND!"

But even the presence of Kostas Michaels, Harrison's

dad, marching down the aisle with two of his bewildered-looking staff carrying platters of food bountiful enough to feed a full house, could not tear anyone's attention away from Charles's performance — except for Kyle, who was following Niko the waiter and digging his hands into the stacked layers of baklava.

Reese shook her head. She had invited him at the last minute but was sort of hoping he would behave. "You are such a pig," she said.

Kyle shrugged and threw his arms around her, planting a sticky, honey-drenched kiss on her left cheek. "I'll make you forget Nolan, baby."

"Ew," said Reese.

"Oooh-la-la!" said Mr. Michaels.

"Thank you, thank you, New York, thank you *all* my fans!" Charles bleated.

Reese grabbed a napkin from one of the platters and scrubbed the side of her face. The stuff was never going to come off.

She glared at Kyle, who was hooting and clapping for Charles, oblivious.

She was glad to be home.

Epilogue

IT WAS DROPPED.

The pilot, that is. Shawn's pilot. The one he had left early for, to shoot in London. The weather there was so bad that shooting was delayed for weeks—and then Fox decided it was too much like some other show on the CW, so they decided not to put it on the fall slate.

You know which show knocked it out of the running? Marisol's. (Ha. Showbiz.)

But that wasn't all. By the time Shawn got back to *Posse Malibu*, his character had been "on vacation in Aspen" long enough that the writers had moved on to some new exciting plotlines that were scoring well in viewer polls, so they decided Shawn's character had died in a tragic avalanche.

I felt for him—Shawn, not his character. He wasn't a bad guy, really. Okay, he was. I did whisper a little *Yes!* when I heard the news. But frankly, I think he'll come out on top. He probably spent the rest of the summer sunning and surfing. He sure didn't spend it contacting me.

You may be wondering:

What was I thinking?

In my worst moments I ask myself that question. And there are a lot of worst moments. But I decided it doesn't pay. It's like asking why does love exist and why does chocolate ice cream with hot fudge and whipped cream taste better to a dancer than celery? You can kill yourself with questions like that.

The important thing is I didn't go.

I almost did, but I didn't.

My mom and dad never totally understood what happened. They saw the flight charge on my Visa bill, but Cousin Ellen and I worked up a story about how my visit had to be canceled due to Ellen's roommate's sudden attack of extremely contagious conjunctivitis. (Her idea, don't ask me—that's why Ellen's on the dean's list, I guess.)

The rest of the summer was not without drama. After the magic show, Mr. Little was good on his promise to reconsider allowing interns to audition for select shows. In fact, he liked the idea so much that he made it a new policy. So Callie was cast in *Guys and Dolls* (beating me out), and Marc got a small part in *Sweeney Todd* over Harrison, which stung. But we pitched in backstage and learned a lot. Brianna finally got her chance to shine in

Fiddler, where she played one of the daughters. She hated her costume but she had the chance to flirt every night with Steve, who had also been cast. In *Fiddler*, almost all of us had little roles—townspeople, Russians, etc. I got to be a guy and wear a beard in the bottle dance. And as for Charles, he was in his element, costuming and choreographing the ushers for each show—dice-rolling gamblers, walking corpses, poor Russian Jews. At the end of the season the Charlushers chipped in and bought him a collection of obscure Broadway show CDs, and I thought he was going to faint.

Dashiell Hawkins was here for the last week of the season. After he showed up for the first two performances, beaming from the fourth row, Mr. Little began comping him, letting him in for free. Although he kept calling him Daniel.

When Dashiell decided to analyze *Fiddler* for Mr. Little one night, scene by scene, I could tell Mr. L regretted the decision.

All in all, it was an amazing summer, but nothing compared with *West Side Story*.

I often wonder what would have happened if Shawn had not been called to London. Would I have ignored my friends and gone? Where would I be now? Every time I turn on the TV and see a new show, or a new character in an old show, I think—what if I had auditioned for that? Would I have gotten the part?

Would I be with Shawn?

Then I force myself to shut up and get real. Instant stardom would have been cool. But even the A-list people take *some* time getting off the ground, doing dozens of auditions every week. And they have driver's licenses. Or parents living in town. I'd be depending on Shawn. *And we know how dependable he is*, I tell myself.

And suddenly I begin noticing the older roles. There are an awful lot of sexy twentysomethings who get the best-looking guys on all the shows. It's okay if it takes a few years before I make it out to L.A.

So when you think about it, the opportunities are looking up. It's a long life.

And in the meantime, there's always senior year.